SURVIVAL IN SAINT PETERSBURG

SURVIVAL IN SAINT PETERSBURG

C.R. PAGE

This book is published by Turn the Page Creations

Findon SA 5023, Australia

Cover designed and created by Alison Page

ISBN 978-0-6454757-6-0

A catalogue copy of this novel is held by the National Library of Australia

First published 2025

To Alison

For indulging my desire to open my mouth for a doughnut, you let me
open my eyes and my mind to an amazing story.

CHAPTER 1

January 2, 2022

EKATERINA

I am Saint Petersburg. I was born in this city, and I will die here. I have never left, not even on holiday. In a few days, I will turn eighty-eight. As the Siege saw the population ravaged through bombing, starvation and hypothermia, I remained. I lost everything and everyone. The city itself was a constant to me, and I was a constant to it.

Pyshechnaya is not usually this busy on a Monday afternoon, but the city's population is always swelled with tourists at New Year's. As someone who has never travelled, I don't know what tourists usually want to see, but I would not think that doughnut shops typically sit at the top of the list. Mind you, tourists might look at me and say senior citizens don't usually spend their days in doughnut shops. Generalisations rarely paint the best pictures.

The best pictures are waiting for people all over this city. Surely, few cities rival our beauty. I hear people refer to Saint Petersburg as the Venice of the North, but I doubt Venice compares. It may have more canals, but is it prettier? It does not have the Hermitage Museum, the Church on Spilled Blood, or the Catherine and Peterhof Palaces. Does it have anything to rival the Mariinsky Theatre? It doesn't have the White Nights. Apparently, of equal significance is that it also doesn't have Pyshechnaya, the doughnut shop that is effectively my second home.

Every person's life is a journey, and every journey is unique. On some journeys, people traverse continents, but mine has rarely spread beyond a few blocks. I do not believe that fact has made my journey less expansive. I have seen and experienced more than most people who have travelled the world could imagine. Few have seen as much as I have. Nobody would wish to have seen all that I have once they understand what my life has entailed.

People come into the shop and look at me curiously. They think I am a mad and eccentric old woman. The thoughts of strangers do not concern me at all. They have no idea of my journey. I live the right way for me, and the views of those who don't understand will not impact that.

I spend as much time as possible here at this time of year. Our winters are bitterly cold, and I have only a tiny electric heater at home. The electricity expense makes this a luxury I cannot afford more than occasionally. Even then, it does little to remove the chill.

Warmth is not the only reason I come here. It is my routine. I arrive at 10 am every morning and stay as long as possible. There is no reason for the time, but I am a creature of routine, and this one dates back further than I can remember. There has always been a feeling of home about this place, far more so than the apartment I've lived in for the past half a century. Home is a feeling more than a place, and Pyshechnaya is where I have that feeling. It symbolises my life like nowhere else.

The staff here have a range of different attitudes towards me. Some of them consider me a problem, with my assistance reducing the need for them and cutting into their hours. Others appreciate having less pressure on them through my help. The varied attitudes do not result in differing behaviour towards me. They might not like my presence, but they consider me fitting to the authentic Soviet-style experience that draws the tourists through the door. There is an acknowledgement of me between the managers and the staff, but nothing more. Like the resident cat, I am a novel part of the furniture.

From my home in a building on Shvedsky Pereulok, it is just a short walk to the shop, and even at my slow pace, it is simple enough. Usually, people are sympathetic enough towards me that they will let me skip the line if there is one stretched outside.

Doughnuts, or pyshki as we call them, are a staple of Saint Petersburg. Anywhere else in Russia, they are called ponchik. This is one of many examples of how we, as a city, are unique, rather than just another part of Russia.

Through the Soviet era, there was very little in the way of fast food. Pyshki was the exception, with many pyshechnye, or doughnut shops, scattered throughout the city. The Soviet economy rejected any form of promotion, so pyshechnye never stood out from each other. While that has evolved in these modern times, my second home at Pyshechnaya retains its Soviet roots. When foreigners learn that the translation of the name of our doughnut shop is '*Doughnut Shop*,' they find it surprising to have such a bland name. That, however, is part of what makes it the institution it has been through sixty-five years of this city's history, which is why these foreigners trek here in the first place.

Sometimes, I see people staring at me, wondering what I am doing here. Do I work here or own the place? Am I a customer or a lonely old woman just trying to avoid the cold? Most of these conversations are had by foreigners. I might not understand a word they say, but throughout life, you learn to read people without needing language.

Of course, most people are too absorbed in their experience to notice who they share space in this world with at any moment. The regulars, as well as the staff, pay little attention to me. I don't carry the same air of mystery to them. I may as well, for although my presence is commonplace, they know little about me. Like any mystery, eventually, people shrug their shoulders and no longer care. Irena, the manager, has been here for years and has never said more than a few words to me. She won't give me a coffee or a pyshki, but neither will she move me along. That, I guess, is enough.

I have one friendship that revolves around this place. A couple of times a week, a man named Yuri comes in. He always buys me pyshki and coffee, and we sit and talk. He lived in the same building as me for many years. For a long time, I knew him by sight but nothing more. Eventually, we began talking and got to know more about each other. Eventually, to my disappointment, he moved house. Rather than destroying our relationship, it became much closer. He had no mother, and I had no son. To some small extent, we began filling those absences for each other. He became more routine about coming to Pyshechnaya, craving the memories from that stage of his life. In our time here, he became the one person who ever got to know my whole life story. With this, he understands why I spend so much of my time here.

He has just arrived, and apparently, we have a job to do. A couple of tourists were here yesterday and wanted to know my story. I'm happy to tell them, but they don't speak Russian, so Yuri will translate.

I used to hate telling anybody about my life, but I'm nearly eighty-eight. What am I hiding? I don't know how much time I have left, and there isn't any legacy I'm leaving behind, so maybe it is best that I tell my story. I'm surprised anyone cares, but as they do, I shall give them what they seek.

CHAPTER 2

January 1, 2022

ADAM

With temperatures ten degrees below freezing, standing in a queue for half an hour to get into a doughnut shop didn't seem like the most sensible way of beginning our time in one of the world's most beautiful cities. Travel isn't always about common sense, as I had to keep repeating to Louise, who was far less enthusiastic about this part of our itinerary than I was.

When travelling as a couple, compromise is imperative. We are 'travel compatible' regarding our desires for similar experiences. Minimal compromise was necessary when we planned our itinerary. We have very little locked in within each destination, preferring to take the city as it comes. I'm willing to cede to Louise by not over-preparing each minute of every day, but I research each destination enough to understand the places I don't want to miss. There were all of the prominent sights in Saint Petersburg, but these would already be handled in the time with our tour group. For our free time in the city, the top of my must-see list was Pyshechnaya.

'Seriously, Adam, travel halfway around the world, and the main thing you want to see is a doughnut shop?' Her response was natural when I showed her my Saint Petersburg wish list a week before we left Australia for our three-month European winter adventure.

'I wouldn't say it is the main thing, Lou. Look at the tour schedule. We already see the Hermitage and the palaces, so I didn't need to put them on my list. This is about unmissable experiences that aren't on the standard tourist itinerary. Pyshechnaya is a more genuine snippet of the authentic city than any tourist site, so it is an integral part of rounding out our time there.'

'More like a way of rounding your body more.'

'The doughnuts are secondary,' I said. 'The experience is what matters. Plus, we're not travelling halfway around the world to visit Saint Petersburg. We are only travelling there from Moscow,' I said. 'Pyshechnaya is one hour out of three months in Europe.'

Travel snobbery is a growing trend. Some people believe that visiting a city's iconic sights is not what authentic travel is about. To them, going to the Eiffel Tower in Paris is too cliched. A real traveller focuses on seeking out the authentic lifestyles of Parisians. They're not entirely wrong, but neither are they entirely right. Travel allows the individual to seek the experiences that will impact them most. Looking purely at the iconic sights gains you very little insight into the realities of a city, but it does provide its own particular level of satisfaction. Balancing this against the actual city of the locals provides the best of both worlds. In this city, the Hermitage is essential, but so too is the city of the locals.

When a local shop becomes famed for its authenticity, there is a danger that it can lose what made it memorable by trying too hard to suit the newfound tourists. Pyshechnaya appeared on several searches as an ideal representation of Soviet-era life when the city was known as Leningrad. I knew this would not typify modern Saint Petersburg life, but it would hopefully be an insight into Leningrad as the locals lived here a generation or two ago.

Hearing Chinese, German, French, English and only a tiny amount of Russian when in the line, it was clear this wasn't the hangout of locals anymore. There seemed to be a few Russian phrase books in hands, as people knew that such an 'authentic' institution as this wouldn't cater to people ordering in foreign languages.

'This is Russia; speak Russian,' I'd heard in a shop the previous day. While the clearly elocuted English statement proved that the speaker could communicate in their customer's tongue, the principle at stake drove him. Fair enough. In the English-speaking world, you are expected to speak our language when dealing with retailers, so why should that not apply here? They are a proud people, proud of their city, nation, and language.

When we joined, the line to get in the door was roughly forty people long. We couldn't speculate how many people were in line inside the door. The movement was just quick enough for us to believe the wait was manageable, and although Louise's patience was tested, I knew she'd cope. She was generally more patient than me, but our tolerance of waiting always depends on what we are waiting for.

'This isn't a doughnut shop, Lou. This place is Saint Petersburg. Pyshechnaya. It is a throwback to the Soviet era and the rebuilding of this city. The line isn't long because of the food. These people are chasing the most authentic Leningrad experience. Every tourist sees the Hermitage and the Church of the Saviour on Spilled Blood and thinks they've seen this city. Think of home. Experiencing Adelaide is less about visiting our Art Gallery or Cathedral than stopping at a 'servo' and grabbing an iced coffee. In Saint Petersburg, the equivalent means eating pyshki; the best place to do that is here.'

Louise thought I was overstating the depth of experience we were getting. She maintained I was seeking a fattening treat. Before arriving here, we had passed numerous doughnut shops, and I was not inclined to settle for any of them. This was not primarily about doughnuts, so there would be no settling for anything other than the original. Whether Louise was now understanding that or merely falling for the smell of the doughnuts, she was starting to get caught up in the moment a little. The shop was so crowded that many people chose to take away their doughnuts, and as they walked past, the smell provided enough motivation to continue waiting, distracting us from how cold we felt.

Once we made it inside, we were disappointed to see that our wait was far from over. We were at the back of a long line snaking through the café. Indeed, the twenty minutes outside was only a third of the overall wait. At least we now had warmth. Well, warmth may be a stretch as the door was continually open to provide the way out for the satisfied customers and the way in for their enthusiastic replacements.

There was very little space in the café. There would have been roughly a dozen tables surrounded by chairs, and all of these were taken. There were several tables against walls where people stood around to eat and chat. These looked far more in keeping with my image of the Soviet-era workers that would have crowded in here long ago. Space by these right now was just as crowded. The line to the counter at the back of the shop trailed between these tables, leaving very little room for anyone.

The shop was opened in 1958, and the tradition and history separated it from the other doughnut shops around the city. The walls in the main dining area were painted in light pink, blue and white vertical stripes that looked far more up-to-date than I'd have expected but covered with traditional Soviet artworks reflecting the values that were respected and expected in society. Pyshki were naturally at the centre of them all.

Every now and then, one of two women in distinctive blue aprons would pass by to clear and wipe a table, but a much older woman was more intriguing. Initially, I thought she was a customer as she was far too old to work here, but possibly things are not like back home. I would have guessed she was ninety, and walking from one table to the next seemed challenging. Whenever a table was vacated, she would take any rubbish and put it in the central bin. She would pile any empty plates or cups on the ledge above the bin. Without the apron, she surely wasn't part of the staff.

'What do you think her story is?' I asked Louise.

'I don't know. Maybe she owns the place.'

'Really? Look at this place, and look at her. It may be cheap, but with this many customers, they still must make a fortune. This woman doesn't look like she has a ruble to her name.'

I noticed her clear a table in the corner where the plate still had half a pyshki. Sure enough, she wasn't letting the pyshki go to waste, so she ate it before moving the empty plate as another couple took the space.

'She's here hoping for the scraps that she will survive off. How sad that life can reach that point,' Louise said.

'Maybe,' I replied, 'though you may find there is much more to her story than meets the eye.'

'Like what?'

'I have no idea. This has been a pilgrimage for me. Maybe she loves doughnuts more than I do, and she is attending her place of worship.'

She rolled her eyes at me. I was fascinated by this woman. She looked like the stereotypical old Soviet woman, plain-clothed, with a head scarf and no teeth. Louise quickly lost interest while I couldn't stop thinking about her. Perhaps she was employed here not so much to clear tables but to provide authenticity to this appearance as a throwback to the Soviet era. If so, they couldn't have found a more suitable option unless they hired a collective of comrades in factory worker attire.

With the prints on the wall showing the Soviet families appreciating pyshki together and the doughnut shop staff bringing people together through these golden fried round delights, perhaps she was just a devotee to the propaganda she'd grown up with. There was no doubt that many of the people here were not just drawn in by the doughnuts but to celebrate nostalgia. For us, it was to see something foreign, but for locals, it was an opportunity to rekindle their youth.

As we approached the end of the line, I repeatedly practised my order in Russian to try to sound like the authentic Soviet man who would have lined up like this a generation ago. I knew I would sound virtually incomprehensible to a Russian, but I always felt better trying, however ordinary the result sounded.

'*Vosem pyshki i dva kofe, pazhaulsta,*' I said nervously while reinforcing with my fingers the number eight for the pyshki and two for the coffees. Whether the lady had understood my attempt at speaking Russian was unclear. With tourists from around the world being much of her clientele, there was always a way of understanding the customer.

There were signs that things had changed a little, with bottles of water and a small range of soft drinks available over the counter. Of course, this divergence from the traditional defeated the purpose of being here, so I wasn't going to entertain any such idea. The coffee may be instant and uninspiring, but as we sought to taste Soviet life, it was best done through the purest possible reflection on the past.

It was not service with a smile, but that made the experience authentic. In Russia, a smile is a deeply personal gesture. It is shared with loved ones, not strangers, not even in customer service. This would only have been more prevalent in Soviet days. Good service here is not about friendliness but efficiency; I couldn't be critical on that score.

The pyshki are more golden in colour than I expected. They are then topped with a liberal coating of icing sugar to add a touch of additional sweetness without heavily impacting the flavour, the way the cinnamon does on a doughnut at home.

We left the counter with a tray holding our pyshki and coffee. The struggle began as we sought a spot in the crowded room to enjoy our order. A couple left a stand-up table in one corner, but before we could get there, the sight of the old woman springing into action had beaten us. She stared back at us, and Louise, fractionally in front of me, stopped suddenly in her tracks. At that moment, the old woman gestured for us to come forward. She had only moved to clear the table for us.

There were no chairs, but that didn't matter. We just wanted to stay inside to appreciate the doughnuts, coffee, warmth, and the place's vibe. Standing leaning at the table seemed the ultimate way of doing this. As we took our place, the old woman was right by us, her heavily lined face showing not just a long life but undoubtedly one that had done things hard. In this city and in that era, I could imagine just how hard.

'*Spasiba*,' I said to thank her and smiled, despite it not being the local custom. She returned a toothless smile. Such gestures were necessary to communicate without a shared language.

There are no serviettes. The substitute used here is a small square of thin paper, thousands of which sit on each table. You pick up the doughnut with the square and eat it without your fingers getting unnecessarily greasy. Serviettes and napkins may be how it would be today, but in a tribute to 1958 Soviet society, little paper squares were the fitting and affordable way.

We surveyed the plate in front of us. Louise was comparing the pyshki to a cinnamon doughnut from home, and as she took her first bite, I could see she was underwhelmed. I took my first bite and was far from disappointed. It wasn't the greatest-tasting treat I had ever known, but it was nice enough. More to the point, it was exactly as it should be. Pyshki may be translated into English as a doughnut, but it doesn't mean that the Russian version is designed to be the same as what we know in the West. The pyshki is crisp on the outside but incredibly light and fluffy on the inside. It has a different taste and texture from the doughnuts I've had anywhere else. I resolve to never again confuse the issue by referring to the pyshki as a doughnut.

Looking across at Louise, I knew immediately what her review would be. 'Yeah, it's alright, but not that special. We'd have been just as good stopping at one of the previous places. I think some of them had more variety, too.'

'Look around you. I think you are missing the point of why we're here. If you believe this experience could be replicated anywhere else, you need to pay attention over the next few days.' Almost protesting her lack of enthusiasm, I reached to the plate, grabbed my next pyshki and savoured the flavour as I bit into it.

Once I felt my point had been sufficiently made, I added that she wouldn't like the coffee much either. While she usually likes proving me wrong, when she took a sip, she couldn't withhold the face that told me I was spot on.

To some extent, Louise and I were the classic pair of customers for Pyshechnaya. For her, it was all about the pyshki, and the cultural experience was a mere by-product. For me, it was the pyshki that was incidental. It isn't what people would expect me to say, for I have a sweet tooth and a well-rounded stomach that is a tribute to a lifelong love of baked treats. The pyshki were memorable, and I would never have been here without them, but I stand by the fact that they remain incidental to the experience. The menu's simplicity, the no-frills, the low-cost approach, the 1950s décor. Every aspect of the café looked like it had barely changed since Pyshechnaya opened more than 60 years ago.

We continued working our way through the plate and our accompanying coffees for the next ten minutes. The whole time, my attention kept returning to the old woman. She sat at one stage, then got up to clear rubbish off tables and intimated to others to take the seats. Eventually, my curiosity became too much, and when one of the staff, clearly identifiable through their blue aprons, walked past, I had to try and find out more.

'Excuse me. Do you speak English?'

She shook her head. *'English, nyet. Russian.'* She walked off, but moments later, another staff member came over, obviously at the first woman's direction.

'Hello,' she said in a heavy accent.

'The old woman over there?' I asked, pointing across the room to where she was sitting in the corner. 'Does she work here? Who is she?'

'She not work here,' the waitress, Natalya, said in broken English, 'But she think she does. I work here for three years, and she here every day. I not know why. Nobody know why.'

With that, Natalya was off again, and the time demands of such a busy place did not allow her to waste time with what would be perceived as tourists asking irrelevant questions. I returned to the plate before me and grabbed my fourth pyshki. Everyone has a unique story, but I was certain hers was more unique and memorable than most. I was desperate to know a little more about it.

While her age showed, her look was stuck in 1958 as that of the cafe. Her clothing was as unremarkable as the Soviet era would have encouraged: a thick, dark-coloured cardigan and a long dark dress that looked like they came from the time of Brezhnev.

A man of a similar age to us had been sitting at an adjacent table. On his way out, he came over, having seen and heard my interest in the old woman.

'Ignore her. She is just a mad old woman. She is just here because she has nowhere else to go. Most people here show interest in one of the other regulars.' He pointed towards the far corner, where an orange cat sat on the table. 'That cat lives here in the shop. Seeing how fat she is, you can probably guess that.'

When researching this place, I'd heard about the cat, though I admit I hadn't noticed her until this local man pointed her out. She'd been hiding in a corner where the line hadn't snaked past. Louise hates cats, so she wasn't interested. I generally wasn't that fond of them. I might have been more interested if the old woman had not dominated my interest immediately. The cat had a story; it was owned here and lived here. Nothing about that seemed unforgettable. The old woman no doubt had a story too, but it had to be far more complex, leading her to a similar presence in this shop as the cat has.

'You know, cats are very special in Saint Petersburg,' the man continued. 'At the war's end, the city was plagued with rats. Cats were specifically brought into the city to combat this issue. There was widespread disease, and the cats' work made the city liveable again. The cat has always had a special place since. Far more than mad women.'

With a nod, he walked toward the door, a slight sneer in the direction of the old woman. There was undoubtedly some history. Perhaps she cleared his table before he finished one time. It seemed the kind of insignificant issue that often causes long-term conflict. Such things worked similarly anywhere in the world.

Natalya walked past again and saw me still looking at the old woman.

'Her name is Ekaterina. I know nothing of her, but one man know her. Yuri. He come here each Tuesday and Saturday about 10 a.m. and talk to her for ages. He speak English. He tell you her story.'

I looked across at Louise as if I was instantly asking permission. She knew that her answer was largely irrelevant, as I would ensure we would be back to get to the bottom of my most significant curiosity about Saint Petersburg.

'Why not?'

Four pyshki had been enough for me, while three had sufficed for Louise. I wondered if Ekaterina would have the last one if I left it. Louise did not like wasting anything, so although I could see she felt she'd had enough, she would stretch herself before I would get the chance to see. Rather than having her regret overeating, I decided to have number five.

It wasn't quiet in the café, but that was unsurprising given the crowds within. Conversations were taking place in many different languages. There were indeed a lot of locals in the place, but they were outnumbered by people who appeared to be from countries across the world. You could see why it was so popular with tourists. Not only was it an opportunity to see a snapshot of Soviet life, but it was also great value. Our eight pyshki and two coffees were less than 200 rubles. We'd pay more than triple for the equivalent at home. I can't imagine they struggle, as they are so busy. In part, the demand is so high because of the low prices. When we found out about this place online, we saw many photos, and I know it isn't always this busy. I assume the morning will be quieter, and as we will be hanging on every word of Ekaterina's story, the reduced noise will be greatly appreciated.

Pyshki finished and the coffees completed, we were both beyond satisfied. People coveting the table space were circling, and we no doubt made someone's day as we got up and left. We walked straight past Ekaterina on our way to the door, and I gave her another smile, which was returned with a nod of acknowledgement.

The line didn't appear much shorter as we came outside. It was close to 7 p.m., just over an hour before closing time. It wasn't really a dinner option, but it seemed sufficient for many, and it had been that for us. Rather than walk to see quite how far the line stretched, we walked the other way towards Nevsky Prospect.

It was still a long walk to our hotel, but having not gone to bed last night in Moscow and then failing to sleep on the train today, we were not going anywhere or doing anything on the way back. If we knew the public transport options, we'd have gone with it, but we were too tired to deal with anything new. Steps, however challenging fatigue made them, remained manageable. We would shuffle on and then sleep like babies. Tomorrow, our deeper discovery of the city begins, but only after our deeper discovery of the life story of Ekaterina.

CHAPTER 3

January 2, 2022

ADAM

We were roughly halfway through a three-month trip to Europe when we arrived in Russia. Moscow and Saint Petersburg had been high on my bucket list for many years, and when we planned the trip, we each had free rein over some choices. Louise was keen to see Russia too, but being somewhere so different in culture and language, she believed it best to visit with the safety net of an organised tour.

'Group tours are not what travel should be. It's so touristy,' I said.

'Touristy shouldn't be such an issue. We are tourists,' Louise said.

'We are travellers,' I said. 'Travellers discover. Tourists are shown. They are part of a group who only see what others choose. You move at their pace, at their whim. It's for people on a trip to rattle off a list of all the famous sights they visited to their friends. What we can experience doing our own thing is far more enriching.'

'It is a little more than ten per cent of our time in Europe. I found one that would be ideal, and it caters to your greatest wish - New Year's Eve in Red Square. It also allows plenty of free time where you can stop being a tourist and have the opportunity to be a traveller.'

Relationships demand compromise. Despite my instinctive protests, I knew there was merit in her suggestion. After researching the tour she'd found and finding it comparatively palatable, I accepted that this was a reasonable time to yield.

Our time in Moscow had eased my reservations. We'd had sufficient free time to explore the city ourselves and then take advantage of the bonuses a tour group provides, skipping lines and gaining additional access to some of the city's best attractions. A country like Russia doesn't attract the most casual of travellers, and the group we were with seemed so much better than what I'd encountered on my first group tour many years earlier.

When we got the train to Saint Petersburg yesterday afternoon, most of the group was a little worse for wear. Louise and I visited the doughnut shop, which was more than most of the group got up to, though a few younger people seemed to manage to revive themselves for a trip out to see some of the local nightlife at the time we were coming back.

Travel seems to be dominated by two main groups: the 18-30 age group trying to discover the world before being tied down, and the 55-plus age group trying to make the most of their time while still physically capable of experiencing all that travel offers. In your early forties, as we are, tour groups are always fraught with danger. You usually end up too old to be able to keep up with everyone else, or too young, and are put to sleep by the rest of the group.

This time, we seem to have struck it lucky. There are 20 travellers in the group, and we are smack-bang on the average age. There are three different family groups, with early 20's kids and their early 50's parents. It is impressive to see the dynamics of these family units and the common ground that allows them to appreciate the same experiences. That said, late at night, there seem to be separate plans for the different generations. In Moscow, Louise and I could easily blend between either subset, though after a few big nights there, I was beginning to feel too old for any group.

'Don't eat much,' I said to Louise, disturbed at her overfilled breakfast plate. We would return to Pyshechnaya at 10 a.m., so I considered that breakfast. I'd mainly come downstairs hoping for a better coffee than I'd get there.

'Breakfast is included, so we may as well make the most of it. It's not like you need to save room for doughnuts. You'll always make room in any situation,' my wife said. Of course, she was entirely correct, but I was conscious that the hotel breakfasts in Russia had been unappealing, particularly in comparison with our previous stops in France and Germany.

Nearly half of this tour was free time. We liked to get out and see the city in our way. The most significant sites in any city had that status for valid reasons. They were well worth seeing, but to understand and feel the uniqueness of a city, it was essential to get away from the tourist path. We liked to walk the back streets, catch public transport, and eat in nondescript places with the locals for part of our time, and we had plenty of chances on this tour.

An optional city tour by bus was being run this morning. We were happy to miss this. We are attending a dinner at a downtown restaurant with the group, but until then, our time is our own. The tour will take us to the Catherine and Peterhof palaces tomorrow and the Mariinsky Theatre in the evening. On Tuesday, we are going to the Hermitage and several of the main downtown sites. We are doing a Metro Station tour on Wednesday, then visiting the Peter and Paul Fortress and Vasilevskiy Island. The only place I had desperately wanted to see in Saint Petersburg that wasn't on the itinerary was Pyshechnaya, and with that now being visited today for the second time, we had the rest of the day to fill with the essence of the city.

Some travellers like to plan every last minute of their trip, while others like to be impulsive and let their destinations dictate what happens. I find myself torn between these approaches. I wouldn't be in Russia if I weren't drawn here by places I wanted to experience. Once I was coming, I had to make sure that time was allocated to do these things. For all of the promise these hold, the most incredible experiences I've had on the road have always been unplanned moments. It is almost a fight with myself not to plan too much, leaving room to find the random gems within a city. I kept looking at my phone for ideas for today, though I didn't want to lock things in. Overplanning takes the magical spontane-ity of a trip away, but unpreparedness can cause you to miss the best highlights. Balance is everything.

Caffeinated, fed to a small extent, and with a plan that consisted of doughnuts, learning the history through the eyes of a local and then the freedom of an afternoon without commitments, we were ready to go.

We decided to walk a different way. A city dominated by waterways warranted walking beside them. It may have been less direct, but we'd left more than enough time for the scenic route. Our hotel was on a cor-ner, and canals ran parallel to both streets. The Griboyedov Canal was taking us in the general easterly direction we needed, so we followed it.

The city feels almost Parisian in parts based on the style of buildings, with businesses downstairs and residences above. We passed more cafes than I could have believed: bars, nightclubs, and stunning architecture. The canal bent opposite a university campus and then headed straight towards the distant sight of the Church on Spilled Blood, its colourful onion-shaped domes perhaps the most iconic image of this city.

We turned at Nevsky Prospect, the city's main thoroughfare. The street rekindles thoughts of Western cities, more Fifth Avenue or Champs Elysees than my preconceived notions of a Russian street. Big companies, high-end fashion, and American fast food combine with the Kazan Cathedral, the Stroganov Palace, and the Alexandrinsky Theatre to make this street an attraction on its own.

'What does it say about you that in a city of such culture and beauty, our first 24 hours here have seen two visits to a doughnut shop?'

'I think it speaks volumes,' I said. 'It says that I can see the culture and beauty that everyone else sees as part of our organised trip, and then I utilise our free time to engage all our senses in the real city. The ballet or the museums aren't the greatest insight into the local culture, how-ever much they can be enjoyed on their own merits. The life experience of someone who has seen everything that this city has gone through in a place where the ordinary local spent their time. That is developing an understanding of the city you're in.'

'So, it's just her story we're going for? You're not getting doughnuts today?'

'I must. We can't sit there and not spend anything, can we? Plus, that's engaging our sense of taste in local culture.'

'I think we've already done that,' she said. Although less enthused than me by the pyshki, I knew she wouldn't decline when they sat before us.

The scene at Pyshechnaya was very different from the previous night. Although the line did not extend outside, it was still snaking its way through the cafe. Ekaterina must have remembered us from last night as she signalled to come over to a table with chairs. She didn't stay, moving on to clear another table, so I joined the queue to get pyshki. As I moved, she saw me and shook her finger, pointing back to the table, so I returned.

Five minutes later, a man in his mid-fifties walked in and went straight up to Ekaterina. He joined us moments later and introduced himself as Yuri. I asked what I could get him and Ekaterina. With their orders confirmed, I made my way to the end of the line, and this time, she nodded her approval.

CHAPTER 4

January 2, 2022

EKATERINA

The Australian man returned with a tray of pyshki and cups of coffee. I hadn't eaten this morning, so I appreciated a pyshki before anything else. I knew they wanted to hear my story, but what exactly did they want to know? Why do I spend my time in Pyshechnaya or something else? Before I began explaining my life, I needed the Australians to explain what they wanted.

'Why are you so interested in her?' Yuri asked them for me.

'I love to people-watch,' the man said. 'I look at people and create detailed pictures in my head of who that person is. However accurate I may be is irrelevant, but when I have the chance to learn more, I love to. When I looked at Ekaterina, all that ran through my head was that she was Saint Petersburg. I know the city has endured more turbulence than any other across the past century. Nobody has lived it all, but I thought she may have seen more of it than most.'

'You know something, you're not too wrong. If all the city has endured could be personified by anyone, it would be Ekaterina. I think she will enjoy telling her story. I'll translate what she says, and then you'll have to tell me if you can believe it.'

'She stretches the truth?' the Australian woman asked.

'No, but truth can be harder to believe than fiction,' Yuri said.

I am like everyone. I view the world through my own experiences. I know I've seen things that nobody should, suffered through traumas you wouldn't wish on a fierce enemy, but that seems normal as it is all I know. Perhaps I could hear their life stories and be equally amazed, for anything they have experienced would be as foreign to me as my story will be to them.

'I don't know if it has been any special sort of life,' Yuri translated moments behind my words. 'I've only lived this one; it is all I know, so to me, it is not special, just life. I shall explain it for you, and you can tell me.'

Their curiosity stems from my looking out of place in the doughnut shop, so I wasn't sure if I should focus strictly on that or explore my life more deeply. I asked Yuri where I should begin.

'The beginning, of course. Eighty-eight years ago. You can't expect people to make sense of where you are today without an understanding of what got you here.'

I wasn't sure how long they'd spend with me, but cramming eighty-eight years into one conversation didn't give scope to being too thorough. I decided I'd just run through everything as I remembered it, adding detail if they looked interested, skipping on faster if their concentration was on the wane.

Born on January 7th, 1934, I was the youngest of Pavel and Olga's three children. My two brothers, Aleksandr and Nikoliy, were born just over a year apart, but there was a decade gap until I came along. I sometimes looked back, wondering if my parents had wanted a third child, based on that time gap, but the events of the next few years made that question moot.

Naturally, my memories of the first couple of years of my life are not pure, but the recollections I have garnered from the stories I heard. Most of these came in the dark days of my childhood, but it was my nature to listen and learn thoroughly. While necessity saw me develop an active imagination, my understanding of the early days of my life predates this. I have no doubts about its accuracy.

We lived in the south of Leningrad, as it was called in those days, with my extended family. My parents, siblings and I shared a home with my Babushka, or maternal grandmother Christina, her other daughter and son-in-law, Yulia and Dmitri, and their two children, Dasha and Anastasia. Ten people in a house may sound cramped, but it was common for extended families to all live together. We were in comparative luxury, as our home had four rooms. Many families as big as ours lived in one-room apartments, part of state-owned high-rise buildings. These were always kept in such poor repair that protection from the elements was minimal. In the cold of our winters, exposure often proved fatal.

Dad and Dmitri had worked hard to ensure that our home was the best protection it could be. They had built an underground shelter, conscious of the need for an extra layer of protection from the elements, but more to protect us from the attacks they feared. We were fortunate to have a separate house, which most frequently was the domain of government officials and bureaucrats. The tremendous communist regime, which worked on the principle of all people being equal, clearly defined who was more equal than others.

'The world is changing,' Dad continually told everyone. 'There will be another World War before too long. The Germans will push outwards and take on the rest of the powers of Europe. We may not be impacted in the initial wave, but at some point, Hitler will either align with us and play second fiddle or attack us. If it's the latter, Leningrad will be the key battleground. If it's the former, the rest of the world will oppose us. With Germany better prepared, they'll see us as the better option to attack first. This will likely come from Finland, and again, it will centre initially on an attack of Leningrad.'

The city's history was significant long before my time on the planet. Peter the Great founded the city in the early 18th century. It coincided with the birth of the Russian Empire and the emergence of our nation as a power. It soon became the empire's capital until the Russian Revolution, when the Bolsheviks returned the capital to Moscow.

The city had been renamed Petrograd to remove the Germanic sound of the historical name. By 1924, the name was again changed to Leningrad in honour of the recently deceased revolutionary leader. Having the permanent reminder of Lenin in our city's name was something we accepted, though, for those of my age, we knew the city far more than the man. However heroic he had been, the Leningrad I was born into endured far too much for me to honour any of the leaders through recent history once I was old enough to learn of them.

My most significant recollection is noise. Ten people in those confined surroundings made a lot of noise. As a baby, I may have been responsible for a fair share of this, but silence required far more than my cooperation. Meals were sacred, and we ate at a table that couldn't accommodate us all but which taught us the bonds of family. Having all you need is not enough if one of your own is going without. That was fundamental to us, and as time passed, the importance of clinging to that belief my father instilled continued to grow.

A new education system was recently implemented to make the Soviet Union the most intelligent nation on Earth. Even at age three, I was at nursery school, my cousins were at kindergarten and primary school, and my brothers were at high school. All of us were learning the need for obedience, hard work and loyalty, qualities fundamental to the society that was being built around us. Aunt Yulia had studied to be a teacher many years earlier, but after the rise to power of the Bolsheviks, the education system had been dispensed with. Stalin had restored this, and there had been such a shortfall in qualified teachers that people like Yulia had been restored to their previous status.

'I too will be a teacher,' Aleksandr proudly said one evening. 'I love Mother Russia and shall serve her by developing the next generation of great Russians.'

Papa shook his head. 'In this life, you need to do what you are told. That doesn't mean you need to believe every word you are told. Mother Russia does a certain amount for you, but she also does much against you.'

Papa and Aleksandr regularly disagreed about issues of the state. The state was said to be responsible for creating the great life we experienced. They both agreed that the state deserved this recognition, but the arguments came when assessing how great this life really was.

'Without understanding the wider world around us, how can you know the value of what we have? Just because the government tells you this is as good as life gets, it is not necessarily true. They communicate the messages that serve their purpose. It should not be taken for granted that these are always accurate.' Papa hadn't experienced much beyond this city, but he had known a wide enough range of people to understand broad perspectives of life's potential. He didn't need a more comprehensive picture to appreciate that it existed.

Papa had been raised in a strongly religious family. The modern state insisted that rejecting religion was as crucial as spurning capitalism, which undoubtedly had driven his anti-government views. His views had formed the basis of our understanding of the world, but with exposure to the thinking of the State through education, Aleksandr no longer appreciated his father's outlook.

'God gave us this world. Men made mistakes that left this world in a dangerous place. Now we have the State run by men telling us that religion, honouring God, has no place. I shall always hold more faith in God than any man,' Papa said.

'God is a creation of capitalists to distract from the evil they do,' Aleksandr said.

Papa didn't push far. However confident he was of the correctness of his views, he knew his son's contrasting beliefs were less dangerous in modern Leningrad. I tried to go with my own interpretation. I saw God as being to society what Babushka was to our household—the one you admire, respect, and look up to, but one who left the daily decisions of your life to the government or, in our family, our father.

At school, I would show loyalty to the State and its teachings. At home, I would join my family in acknowledging God and his teachings. Maybe one day, these two views would move a little closer together.

Many people refer to their childhood years as the happiest of their lives. Even those who experience tragedy through this stage usually file memories that focus on the most joyful times so that the childhood memory is happier than the reality had been. I cannot recall genuine happiness from my childhood. There were moments when life's problems seemed to only exist outside the door. A knock on that door would begin the fundamental issues that impacted us.

CHAPTER 5

January 2, 2022

ADAM

Reading history in a book or seeing it on a screen can shock and disturb you, yet the impact only cuts so deep. The significance is more profound when you get a more immediate view of it in a direct conversation with someone who has lived it. Everything we see in Saint Petersburg would now be seen through the filter of Ekaterina's experience.

'Where to?' Louise asked, unsure whether we should look to delve deeper into the disturbing elements of the stories Ekaterina had told us or to seek the uplifting opposite side to the city.

'Let's just walk and see what we see.'

We found the Museum of Soviet Arcade Machines. Although curious, the cost was enough to suggest it needed a couple of hours to justify entry, so we kept walking. Straight after this was the Church on Spilled Blood. We couldn't walk past the city's most famous landmark even though we knew it was on our itinerary later in the tour.

'I haven't updated my social media profile pics for a few days,' Louise said. 'This should be the ideal spot.' We took a couple of selfies and photos of each other and made ourselves look quite the tourists. All the souvenir sellers had us right in the frame immediately. They started offering us 'great bargains,' their English extending to anything that would help them to make a sale.

We walked up the embankment to the first bridge and came down the other side, seeing the church from the other side. The top dome was surrounded by scaffolding, which cheapened the sight, but it is an inevitable part of travel. When we started our trip to London, Big Ben was hiding behind it. Rarely can you go to a city full of older attractions and not find at least one obstructed by the critical need to protect and conserve.

We continued on the embankment, crossing the Moyka River and found ourselves in the Field of Mars. A green park, its main attraction was a central memorial honouring the victims of the Russian Revolution of 1917. After all we had heard this morning, it was easy to forget that the history of this city was incredibly turbulent long before Ekaterina's time. The winners write history, and the memorials in this city tend to focus on the parts of history that suit them. The victims of the revolution were more worthy of honouring than some of the later political victims, at least in the opinions of those who dedicated such memorials.

At the end of the Field of Mars, we were right by the banks of the Neva River, the city's main waterway. The Troitsky Bridge linked the central part of the city to the Petrogradskiy District, while further to the left, we could see the Peter and Paul Fortress dominated by the cathedral spire.

We walked right, heading along the banks of the Neva, past the Summer Garden on our right. It was unseasonably comfortable for this time of year. Though we needed the multiple layers we wore, walking alongside the river wasn't freezing us as anticipated. The city's waterways were often frozen by this point of the year, but that wasn't the case at this stage. The standard conditions dictated the ability of vessels to be out there, with no boats anywhere on the city's waters at this time.

Across the road was a long row of apartment buildings. 'Imagine the view from the top levels,' I said. At the end of these was a smaller building, which, after a check on my phone, housed the coffee museum.

'Do you want to go in?' I asked.

'I'm not sure Russia is the place for a coffee museum,' she said. 'From my experiences, a vodka museum would make more sense.'

'We're going there with the tour group on Friday.'

We decided to keep walking, and soon after, we came across two sphinxes. Both of these were emaciated. Their ribs were jutting out, and their faces showed bare sculls. The sphinxes were looking across the river, straight at the Kresty Prison, where many of the Leningrad victims of the Purge were sent to on the way to their final punishment.

'This is it,' I said.

'What?'

'The memorial to the victims of political repression.'

Louise gave me a puzzled look.

'The purge, predominantly,' I said to Louise.

'What was the purge?' she asked.

Ekaterina was thorough about all she had experienced but didn't go into the greater context of moments, which was reasonable. We'd asked for her story, and it was the personal impact that she gave us, not the broader perspective of the history of Saint Petersburg.

'I don't know much about it, but it was before World War II and Stalin joined the Allies. At that stage, his concern wasn't the security of Russia from foreign powers, but holding his power from internal opposition. He feared anyone who opposed him and had them taken care of, whether by imprisonment or execution. There were no trials, just results. Kill a million and scare a hundred million more into following you through anything.'

'Why isn't more said about this?'

'It's not a secret. Well, here it probably is, to an extent. History is full of tragedies that are rarely discussed. Still, it showed in Moscow how revered Lenin remains, while there is significantly less memorialising Stalin. In the West, we think about him not as much as Hitler's great rival but as a similar figure. They both committed the worst atrocities on their compatriots. In Hitler's case, it was racial, but for Stalin, it was just about retaining power, the basest urge of any political figure.'

'At least Stalin was pivotal to stopping Hitler. He deserves recognition for that.'

'That is circumstantial rather than a point of great credit. Stalin looked to join Hitler rather than the Allies, but Hitler was too ambitious. If the Nazis had made the right call and allied with Stalin, we would live in a very different world today. That is if we existed at all.'

It was a depressing topic, but avoiding it in this city was impossible. As much as it impacts your thinking, you can't fully appreciate the beauty of this city without understanding the other side. The tragedy and the ability to overcome it make the city triumphant. This triumph and resilience has turned the turmoil into what it is today.

'Can you imagine anywhere that has seen so much loss of life being given such a small memorial?'

Louise shook her head. When you make the ultimate sacrifice in a war, you are forever honoured, but when you make the same sacrifice while recognised as an enemy of your state, you are forgotten. This city was home to vast numbers from both categories, though most of the latter were not true enemies. In many cases, they did nothing to show any opposition to Stalin's government. All that was required was to be perceived as a threat. When the government was so mired in the fierce protection of its power base, it took little before any person was seen as an opponent.

'You know, the Purge is often called the Great Terror. Think of all the modern-day terror we have seen in our lifetimes. That's what these people were the victims of. Just because the official government was behind it doesn't make the action any less appalling. I guess it's a victory that there is any memorial here, but it is so small and subtle that most people will never see it as an acknowledgement of it being an act of state-sponsored terror.'

'We should have had Yuri with us to translate,' Louise said. There were a lot of words engraved on the memorial in Russian. A quick internet search revealed that these were quotes from writers, including Solzhenitsyn, who were also victims of repression.

'He wasn't a victim of the Purges, so I guess this memorial is for more than just those victims. I guess that probably further validates the fact that The Purge isn't acknowledged. One of the great ironies is that many people associated with the church were targeted.'

'Ironic?'

'Yeah. What are the symbols of this country? Saint Basil's Cathedral, Saint Isaacs and the Church on Spilled Blood. Religion is a huge part of the country's iconography, yet the government felt threatened and sought to destroy it. Fortunately, while they stripped its role, they didn't destroy the buildings, so once views changed, the infrastructure was in place. Imagine if they'd lost the history.'

'Do people here know much about that?'

'Clearly, Ekaterina does.'

CHAPTER 6

March 1938

EKATERINA

Mama was always nearby. If she was out of sight, then almost certainly Babushka would be there. The other children and I were always safe between the two women and Aunt Yulia. Papa and Uncle Dimitri were always at work. They left home before I woke up and were gone until supper. Supper time was always the best part of the day. Not only did we have the best meal, but we had everyone together as a family. As the family's baby, I just sat and stared at everyone. Sometimes, I would make faces at my cousin Dasha, who was just a few months older than me, but more frequently, we'd be separated as they couldn't trust us to behave together.

One evening, there was no supper. Babushka brought us something to eat, but Mama and Papa were nowhere to be seen. I heard Aleksandr and Nikoliy discussing this but couldn't understand what they said. I didn't have the words to express strong enough emotion, so tears were all I could offer in the fear and confusion surrounding the break from routine. Babushka comforted me, or at least tried to, but by this point, it wasn't food nor the ceremonial nature of the meal I wanted. I just wanted my parents.

Eventually, Mama and Aunt Yulia came to help Babushka with Anastasia, Dasha and me.

'Your fathers have gone away for a while. We had to help them get prepared. Everything will be alright, but it will be a while before we see them.'

Aunt Yulia ran out of the room crying, and only Mama was strong enough to look out for all of the children while Babushka tried to comfort Aunt Yulia. We, of course, took the words we heard at face value. We didn't consider why my older brothers weren't being told all this. They might not have been told the truth, but they were aware enough that they couldn't be fed lies with no credibility.

Again, there was no sitting together for supper the next night. Mama was there, and after a while, so too was Aunt Yulia. We were fed like usual, but the noise was missing. Only Anastasia, Dasha, and I made any noise, while everyone else remained quiet and sad. Everyone missed my father and Uncle Dimitri, but I didn't understand why they made such an issue of being away for a short time.

The following week, we were back sitting around the table for supper. Papa and Uncle Dmitri were still not back home, so there were just the eight of us.

'When is Dad coming home?' Dasha asked while waiting for her meal.

'You will not discuss that at the table,' Aunt Yulia swiftly replied.

'Because he isn't coming back,' Aleksandr said.

'Aleksandr, get out,' Mama said.

'Many things are happening in this city right now,' Babushka said. 'We don't know how long before we will see your fathers, but if you have more questions, then there is a time and a place for them. The supper table is a happy place, and we are only to talk about happy things.'

That stuck with me forever. When you share food around a table, it is a happy place. You discuss happy things. You reflect and celebrate the past, plan for the future, and find the best parts of the present to share with your loved ones. Babushka may have known more about our fathers than she would tell us, but it would never come out at mealtime.

I slept in a room with the other four children. Usually, the younger three would be asleep before my two brothers came in, but one night, I woke up and couldn't get back to sleep. I didn't cry out and have Mama's attention, but I was lying awake when Nikolaiy came in.

'Where is papa?'

'You should be asleep,' Nikolaiy said. 'Questions like that should be asked of Mama. Or maybe Aleksandr.'

Aleksandr followed soon after, and I asked him the same question about our father.

'He is with Uncle Dmitri,' my eldest brother said.

'But where?'

'When you are older, you will understand.'

'I want to know. Where is he?'

Aleksandr refused to give me an answer. He got Mama, telling her I was awake and crying. She came in, and I said the boys refused to tell me where Papa was, but I felt sure they knew.

'We always want to know all the answers, but sometimes we must wait. It is often much worse to know part of the answers when they don't make sense. The boys don't know, none of us do, but we worry more because we know a little. We are protecting you. We will tell you when we know exactly where they are and when we will see them again. Between now and then, we pray and hold close those we love and have here.'

She hugged me tight, and I faintly heard her sobbing as she did. I wanted to ask her why, but my eyes grew heavy quickly, and I was into the world of dreams where the entire family was at the supper table.

A few days later, Archpriest Vasily came to the house. He had been a regular visitor to the house throughout our lives. Mum had taught me that he was a holy man who was very important but that some of the influential men in the government didn't like him. When she was a girl, everyone would go to churches to listen to men like Archpriest Vasily, but that was no longer happening in the Soviet Union. He now spent more time seeing those people in their homes, and his visit to us was like his visit to so many others.

He prayed with the adults, then talked closely with Aleksandr and Nikolaiy. He spoke cheerfully to Anastasia, Dasha, and me. I asked him why he was visiting us.

'I am just making sure that all of you are all right,' Archpriest Vasily said.

I had seen Mum and Aunt Yulia both in tears when he'd prayed with them, so he was not making them feel better. I knew it had something to do with the men of the house, but as usual, I didn't get a response to any questions I asked. Over the coming months, I asked less frequently, but the answers never changed. Eventually, I'd overheard enough different things that I would no longer ask generalised questions.

'Mama, what is the Purge?'

For the first time, instead of running to her crying daughter, she ran crying from her daughter. Babushka came in, and I told her what I had said. I explained what I had overheard at different times.

I had just turned four years old and had a life lesson that most children will never have. As a family, we sat together while Mama and Aunt Yulia told us everything they knew, most of which Babushka and the boys already seemed to understand. Mama didn't know with certainty what fate had befallen Papa and Uncle Dmitri, but she knew the first part of what had happened. The government's secret police, the People's Commissariat of Internal Affairs, had arrested them. Archpriest Vasily had brought information suggesting they had been sent to a Gulag labour camp. No news had filtered back from there, however, it had been confirmed that several people arrested the same night as Papa and Uncle Dmitri had been shot before leaving the city.

In time, it was apparent that vast numbers died at the Gulag through starvation, disease, exposure and experimentation conducted on prisoners while helping develop the nation's armed forces. In many cases, no bodies were ever identified, and no evidence of death was provided. This was what we faced.

We never saw Papa and Dmitri again. There was never a point where I accepted they had been killed, but day by day, the hopes of a return faded further from my thoughts. Eventually, I stopped thinking about them in anything but the past tense.

What they endured was forever unknown. Whether they were executed immediately or went through the range of torment exposed at the Gulag camps, they were amongst the millions of Soviets who died at the hands of our nation. They were treated as state criminals without ever committing an offence. No evidence existed, but none was needed. They may have opposed the government but weren't actively involved in anything political. Perhaps they spoke to the wrong person at the wrong time, for that would be all it would take.

The Great Purge saw approximately a million Soviets die, more than 40,000 in Leningrad. In many cases, these were people arrested purely to aid arrest quotas being reached by the secret police. There were no fair trials, and much of the action was taken away from the public eye, using the cover of night. Years earlier, Stalin had passed laws that had eliminated the ability for people found guilty of terrorism to appeal. The requirements needed to convict someone on terror were negligible, and high-ranking figures who had opposed Stalin were quickly arrested, tried, convicted and executed before people knew anything about it. Our family were insignificant minor characters in this, but a personality clash with the wrong person had brought us to the attention of the NKVD, the feared government agency for internal affairs. From that moment, freedom was never going to last.

Mama never acknowledged the finality of it. She prayed for Papa as long as she lived. Despite understanding no part of what had happened, I knew I would never see him again. Given the losses to come, perhaps it was in my best interest to learn about coping with the loss of people you love at such an early age.

CHAPTER 7

January 2, 2022

ADAM

We walked along the embankment of the Fontanka River and noticed an elaborate palace on our right.

'No wonder there was an uprising,' Louise said. 'How many palaces did these people need?'

Although we have not visited any of them, we will see the Catherine and Peterhof Palaces tomorrow. We passed the Marble Palace earlier this morning and were headed towards another on Nevsky Prospect later on our walk.

'I'm sure they would all have been built at different times and for different purposes, but it seems excessive in a place where the masses had to live without. There is incredible opulence here compared with Moscow. That is why the revolutionaries were determined to make Moscow the capital. It is far more representative of what they believed in.'

The palace was a striking building that now houses part of the Russian Museum, focusing on Russian artists. We didn't consider going in and proceeded to the adjacent Mikhailovsky Garden. Any English publication related to Russia was often strange in how it anglicised names. The palace and the gardens could be called Mikhailovsky or Michael, yet our guidebook was sufficiently indecisive to have used one of each. In some instances, I was getting confused into the thought that these were two different places.

We spent an extended period taking advantage of the green space. A trail ran alongside the Moyka River at the far end. The Field of Mars, where we had been earlier, was just across the river from us. After following the riverside trail, we returned to the other side and found ourselves just across from the Church on Spilled Blood, the domes of which gave us our bearings back. It was probably a more beautiful place in summer, or maybe even under a decent dusting of snow, but the essence of travel is that you often only get one impression of a place, and this was our time.

After almost an hour, we were back where we had entered the gardens. We made our way back down to the Fontanka River. We crossed over at the first bridge and along the embankment towards Nevsky Prospect. As lacking in confidence as I was about my bearings, I thought this would get us towards the Anichkov Bridge.

One of the most famous monuments in Saint Petersburg, the four-horse tamer sculptures sit on the corners of the Anichkov Bridge. The four different sculptures depict man and horse together, ranging from one with the man walking the horse, to the horse taking control, to the man being nearly defeated, and finally, the man regaining control. The sculptures appeared soon after the bridge was rebuilt in the mid-19th century. Originally, a bridge was built much earlier, the first in the city and featured in Pushkin and Dostoevsky's works. The sculptures were removed from the bridge during the Nazi attacks of the 1940s when the bridge was under heavy bombing. They were buried inside the gardens of the Anichkov Palace. Some of the impact of the attacks prompted this move, as there are visible remnants of artillery fire on one of the statues.

Horse statues are prominent in this city. Catherine the Great commissioned the Bronze Horseman statue, the city's most famous work of art. This statue sits in Senate Square near Saint Isaacs. One of Pushkin's most famous works was a poem titled The Bronze Horseman, inspired by the statue.

At either end of the bridge was another palace. The Anichkov Palace was a Baroque-style palace built for Empress Elizabeth. It had remained with the crown until the October Revolution. Across the river was the Beloselsky Palace, a French-designed building constructed just after the bridge was completed. The palace is now the city's property, and its elaborate interior is often used for exhibitions and concerts.

From the bridge, we could see the obelisk in the distance. Although I wasn't sure, I believed it was a memorial for the Siege, so we made our way east along Nevsky Prospect. It was roughly three blocks before we arrived at Ploschad Vosstaniya, which translates to Uprising Square.

Louise pointed across the square to Moskovsky Rail Station. 'That's where we arrived, isn't it?'

We hadn't come out this way and seen the obelisk, walking through a side entrance to a bus that had taken us to our hotel. This was all new scenery, but the station had been the terminus. It had been pouring rain then, so we'd rushed to the bus without thinking of our bearings. Ironically, the train ran from Leningrad Station in Moscow to Moscow Station in the former Leningrad.

'I think it makes perfect sense,' Louise said. 'Why call it Leningrad Station in Leningrad? You know you are in Leningrad. By calling it Moscow Station, you know that is where you go if you want to go to Moscow.'

'Does every train at Moscow Station go to Moscow?'

'How would I know? But most European cities have a few different major stations for intercity trains. Maybe there is also a Finlandsky Station for trains that run across the Finnish border.'

The obelisk dominated the centre of the square. It was roughly fifty metres high, and the main feature was its crowning with a gold star. The star was designed to represent the status bestowed upon Leningrad as a 'hero city.'

'Ekaterina referred to that title. She said it was embraced by many people who had fled the city for safety and then returned. Those who stayed throughout the Siege had done what was needed rather than talked about it,' Louise said.

'Isn't that visible everywhere? It's amazing how many lifelong loyal fans a football team has when winning. When all is going disastrously, they are nowhere to be seen. When the crowd numbers have trebled once the victories begin, all of them claim to be in the minority that were there all along. The ones who yell about it loudest are usually the ones who jumped on board last.'

'This is a bit higher stakes.'

'Absolutely, but the same principle applies,' I said. Of course, if I were in that situation, I would have escaped the city when I could. I also would have recognised the city, not my place in it, as heroic when all was said and done.

This square was significant in the revolution, with the Bolsheviks renaming it Uprising Square in 1918. At that time, the Church of the Sign was the main feature of the square, but in the era when the church was considered an enemy of the state, it was demolished, replaced in time by the main hall of the Ploshchad Vosstaniya metro station, which ended up here.

Now, for all of the impact of the heavy traffic passing through and for the prominent buildings surrounding it, Ploschad Vosstaniya is known predominantly for the obelisk. As much as a symbol like this was needed after the war, it wasn't until 1985 that it was installed.

The battle for Leningrad was one of the key reasons behind the Red Army setting the Germans back. As much as Britain and America celebrate their roles in victory through World War II, it was the Soviet Union who made the most sacrifice and developed the deepest inroads through the Axis. The war could not have been won without the Red Army, and the Red Army could not have defeated the Germans without the resilience of all involved at Leningrad. It indeed was a hero city.

CHAPTER 8

September 1941

EKATERINA

At the end of the war, Leningrad was considered a hero city. Nobody could have envisaged what the city would experience a few years earlier.

My father predicted war, and he was proven right. His ability to understand what would happen may have contributed to his being brought to the authorities' attention.

War had broken out in other parts of Europe a couple of years earlier, but we in the Soviet Union were not involved initially due to a non-aggression agreement. The Germans broke this with their invasion of our nation in June.

The Siege of Leningrad began in September 1941, when I was seven. It lasted for 872 days. For that period, the city and everyone within it experienced true hell. In many realms, children are protected from life's most atrocious horrors, but during the wartime in Leningrad, there was no way of hiding us from anything.

872 painstaking days. It seemed like decades for most people, but for someone of my age, it became all I knew of life. We remained in our small home on the city's outskirts, but now we were all confined to the tiny basement most of the time. Although the basement was suitably sized for two or three people, it had to accommodate eight of us at the beginning of the Siege.

Many families had left Leningrad before the beginning of the Siege, but the theoretical security of our basement had convinced our family to remain. While these convictions had an element of truth, their decisions were built around best-case scenarios. Hundreds of thousands fled Leningrad in the summer of 1941, fearing what was to come in the ensuing months. For those who waited, it became too dangerous to leave once the bombings began in August. I was sure the adults believed the blockade would only last a short period, and then freedom would be ours. With hindsight, I suspect they felt annihilation was equally likely, but it would be quick. In that instance, any escape to the north that others were taking would not have led to a more secure future. If the Nazis overran Saint Petersburg, they would likely march on, continuing to conquer.

By September, the Germans had surrounded the city, and any last chance of evacuation had now passed. Not only was it impossible to leave the city, but we also faced the reality that nothing, most notably food, could enter the city. Rationing began, and we were all forced to live off the tiny amounts each of us was entitled to. To supplement these rations, Aleksandr and Nikoliy joined the city's defence. They were still just boys, yet during the Siege, boys had to become men before their time.

My brothers' primary task was to put out fires started by German bombs. Firefighting is always dangerous, but it was far more so in this case. Not only were the fires themselves a source of danger, but they were also facing the constant threat of further bombing barrages.

How often we saw the boys varied. Sometimes, they would come home with additional treats they'd managed to source. While we were living off little more than a couple of slices of bread per day, anything extra was considered a treat. Other times, the boys were sent further across town and would be gone for several days. With all the carnage throughout the city, every absence resulted in fear and anxiety within the household. While I was too young to appreciate this then, the memory bank tends to distort such things. I feel like I was waiting by the door for their return, yet I know I was oblivious to the risks at such a young age. Where the boys went and what they did was a source of jealousy. I was couped in the basement, obviously out of necessity, but for reasons beyond my understanding. As I saw it, the boys enjoyed being outside, seeing sunshine and breathing fresh air.

Of course, the truth was far different.

One night, Aleksandr came home with extra rations. This would typically be seen as something extraordinary, yet the mood remained sombre. Other than my young cousins, nobody said anything. I didn't even notice Nikoliy come home. When Aleksandr was still at home all day the next day, I asked where Nikoliy was.

'You have to ask Mama,' he said.

I was seven. Of course, I didn't understand why I needed Mama to tell me something he could easily do himself. I also asked Babushka, but she wouldn't answer me. It was the next day before I saw Mama, who seemed to be in hiding.

'He has gone to be with your father,' she told me.

I had never understood where my father was. I was too young to understand what was happening now, let alone when Papa was taken. I knew I would never see my father again, so I assumed that this meant I would never see Nikolaiy either.

How well can moments be remembered after eighty years have passed? I am not sure, but I don't think I cried. I believe circumstances had already taught me that these things happen. Tragedy is just a part of life. We do what we can to avoid it, but once it happens, we move on. I was born as one of ten people in this household. Courtesy of the people with power on both sides of the conflict, it was now down to a family of seven, and I was still months shy of my eighth birthday.

There were no celebrations for my birthday. I don't think any of us knew when the day had come. Leningrad in January is freezing, and with no power, heating, or food, survival could not be taken for granted. Moreover, bombs continued to rain on our city.

Aleksandr would leave in the dark every day to help protect the city and return with whatever he could muster. It was still so soon after losing Nikoliy that we'd yet to come to terms with the risks Aleksandr was taking. One day, he kissed my cheek as he left in the morning and never returned. Eighty years later, I can still feel his lips on my cheek, and I can still see his smile as he walked away, saying that he would see me that night.

When he hadn't returned home in 24 hours, we all knew what must have happened. Even at my age, I'd been exposed to enough that I no longer was protected by ignorance. Mama ventured out to try and seek answers. Eventually, she found Rudi, a family friend who verified that he was one of five victims of a bomb that had exploded less than a mile from our home.

Hitler had set the destruction of Leningrad as the chief goal of his Northern Army. Aligned with Finland, he planned to set an example with the complete destruction of the city and the transfer of all land north of the Neva River to the Finns. The plan was for his army to completely encircle the city, allowing no routes in or out and to bomb the city sufficiently to destroy infrastructure. Starvation was a significant part of his plan, so food stores were a major target for the bombings.

German intelligence had suggested that starvation would take hold in a matter of weeks without food supplies being able to get into the city. They didn't want the trouble and expense of relocating or feeding the population. They would refuse surrender from the citizens of Leningrad, wanting them destroyed through their own lack of means. The Nazi Army would march into the city, celebrate the victory and then raze every last reminder of what had previously stood. It may be an urban legend, but there are stories that invitations had been printed for a victory celebration in downtown Leningrad before the city was razed. Other suggestions include rebuilding the city as a northern outpost of the Third Reich named Adolfsburg, but most of the planning indicated nothing more than destruction.

Mum, Babushka and Aunt Yulia would take turns venturing through the streets to claim their rations and to attempt to make trades where suitable. For us three girls, a trip above ground was infrequent due to the danger involved. The damage didn't take long to see, as the entire front section of our house had fallen. Rubble provided additional protection for the basement, but this would be insignificant if the front line got to us and beyond. Luckily the work of civilians, including my late brothers, had provided trenches and fortifications to stall the advances of the Nazis. Given their long-term strategy, they didn't feel compelled to move in on us, feeling sure we couldn't survive long anyway.

Winter in Leningrad can see temperatures reach as low as minus thirty degrees. As well as targeting food supplies, Nazi bombings had also ensured that energy supplies had been decimated, ensuring that there was no heating. We all wore every possible item of clothing and remained under multiple layers of blankets. We stayed cold, but at least not to the point of hypothermia. By the end of 1941, it was estimated that a million people had fled the city, and another half a million had died. People trying to escape were killed in bombings, and those remaining died of starvation, hypothermia, and the ongoing German attack. The three women making decisions in our lives knew that survival was unlikely, whatever option they chose. With the city surrounded, escape seemed impossible. As likely as the complete extermination of our city appeared, staying remained our most reasonable hope of survival. The war was being fought on so many fronts; if the Germans were under enough threat on other fronts, perhaps they would be forced to retreat here. That slither of hope made the decision simple for our family.

Even water was a problem. The temperatures had been so cold that all the pipes across the city were frozen, and people's taps had run dry. The population was thirsty as well as hungry. People wandered with buckets in search of water. In some cases, they walked out onto the rivers, searching for holes in the ice where they could get any small amount of water.

In December, 53,000 people died in Leningrad. A small number of these were from German bombs. For most, it was death from starvation. Nobody could imagine at this stage that this would be the same scenario we would face the next year and the one after. No city could survive such a hell for such a length of time.

For the Germans, there was too much to gain in Leningrad. It was geographically strategic, symbolically important, and as was the style at the time, an opportunity to fund its nation through looting the city's wealth. Leningrad was home to invaluable art through its palaces and museums. The Bolsheviks had already seized the Imperial Faberge Easter Eggs in the October Revolution. No doubt the Nazis would be looking for these.

CHAPTER 9

January 2, 2022

ADAM

I shouldn't have been surprised. Louise's lack of enthusiasm at the earlier options of a coffee museum and an arcade games museum was utterly opposite to her attitude when we stumbled across the Faberge Museum. Housed in yet another palace, the Shuvalov Palace, the museum was a stunning building with a beautiful outlook on the Fontanka River across the road.

While I had heard of Faberge Eggs, I didn't know much about them, except that their price tags meant they were for few people other than the tsars. Peter Carl Faberge created them at the request of Tsar Alexander III. As many as sixty-nine of these eggs were made, fifty-two of which were imperial eggs, produced for either Alexander or his heir Nicholas II. Both tsars gave these as gifts for their wives and mothers.

The Faberge Museum was established by one of Russia's wealthiest men, Viktor Vekselberg, who bought more than a dozen eggs from an American who previously owned them. Vekselberg spent more than $100 million on the nine imperial eggs he purchased because he believed they should be displayed in Russia. Along with the acquisition of as many other Faberge products as he could accumulate, the basis for the museum in Saint Petersburg was established.

As much as there was beauty in every corner of the museum, the emphasis was on the Blue Hall. Here, the nine imperial eggs are featured, each a masterpiece of jewellery, art and creativity. Each transcends its place within a collection by being its own special and unique piece of history.

Hen is the oldest of all Faberge eggs, made in 1885. It was initially intended to be one of a kind, but the Tsar and his wife loved it so much that Alexander asked Faberge to produce new ones for him each year.

Renaissance was the last easter egg commissioned by Alexander III before his death. It is adorned with rubies and diamonds and has a gold frame. Its surprise inside was lost many years ago, and it is uncertain what this may have been. Some speculate it was pearls, while it is also commonly thought that another egg, the Resurrection, was the missing surprise. This had been considered a separate Faberge egg, but its curvature has it fit perfectly in the Renaissance and has similar decorations.

Rosebud was the first Easter egg Nicholas II gave his wife, Empress Alexandra, in 1895. It is made of striking red enamel and features a portrait of Nicholas and the date on top. The surprise was a yellow rosebud, referencing the tea rose so prolific in Alexandra's original home of Darmstadt.

The Imperial Coronation was designed as a tribute to the empress who would receive it. The egg is gold with an array of diamonds on its top and another cluster at its narrower bottom. The surprise was a 10-centimetre-long replica of the imperial coach that had carried Alexandra to her coronation.

Lilies of the Valley is an art nouveau-style egg topped with rose-pink enamel featuring gold, diamonds, rubies, and pearls. The surprise comes out of the top of the egg and features three portraits: one of Tsar Nicholas and one of each of his two oldest daughters.

Cockerel features a clockface and resembles a creation of centuries earlier, capturing more of a 17th-century French style. The surprise is a singing cockerel with natural feathers that emerges from the top of the egg, opening its beak and flapping its wings.

Fifteenth Anniversary was my favourite of the eggs. The egg was made of white, green and gold enamel and decorated with diamonds.

There were sixteen panels on the egg, each of which featured a picture relevant to the fifteen-year reign of Alexander III. Included in this was the opening of the Alexander III Bridge in Paris, the procession to his coronation, his daughter and his son. The detail in each panel was incredible, and while less spectacular from a jewellery perspective than some of the other eggs, its additional degree of history gave it an extra impact on me.

Bay Tree looked far less like an egg and more like an ornamental tree. While the anniversary egg was gifted to Alexander's wife, this one was presented to his mother. It was bigger and filled with a broader array of jewels, and it has the surprise of a feathered songbird that flaps its wings and sings when a tiny lever is turned.

Order of Saint George was amongst the last Faberge eggs made. It was presented in 1916 during the First World War. In keeping with the time, it was one of the more austere eggs made. It commemorated the Order of Saint George awarded to the tsar. He presented the egg to his mother, and it survived with her when she fled for Kyiv just before the Bolsheviks took the city.

'I like this one best,' Louise said as we moved towards the eggs made for people other than the tsars. The Duchess of Marlborough Egg had caught her eyes. The Duchess of Marlborough had travelled to Saint Petersburg in 1902 and attended a ball at the Winter Palace. It is believed she saw the collection of eggs belonging to the empress and thought that she deserved such an item, not realising how exclusive they were. Her egg looks like a miniature antique vase on a pedestal. The shell is pink under a combination of gold, silver, pearls and diamonds.

We moved through the other rooms more quickly, knowing that we were due to meet our tour group at dinner in a couple of hours. Uncertain of our way around the city, we knew we couldn't afford to cut things too fine.

The gold room featured more miniature figurines, the white room had jewellery boxes and dishes, and the red room had vases, candelabras and tea sets. Every component of the museum highlights luxury and the best of craftsmanship. Still, the eggs elevate this from a mildly interesting exhibit to a worthy itinerary item for anyone in this city.

Their beauty didn't impact me as much as it did Louise's, but I couldn't help but be intrigued by the history behind each creation. History itself doesn't usually fascinate me greatly, but perhaps our interaction with Ekaterina has personalised every component of this city's history for me.

However beautiful all we saw here was, it felt hard to reconcile that a quarter of a century after these eggs were being made at the cost of a king's ransom, most of the remaining citizens here would have given anything for a couple of slices of bread.

CHAPTER 10

January 1942

EKATERINA

Usually, it was my mother or my aunt who went out to collect our rations. It was a risky task, but as children, we took what they did for granted. We never had enough to eat, but we always had something at our ultimate point of desperation, thanks to one of the adults taking their chances above ground. Sometimes, this would take an hour, while they may line up for ten hours other times. In winter, the wait could lead to death through exposure. The worst part of the wait was the lack of certainty that it would be worthwhile. The principle of rationing was to ensure that the small volume of available food was shared, but sometimes, there was not enough to allocate to everyone. You could wait all day and find nothing was left when it came to your turn. Or you could get food only to face the threat of being mugged by someone who had missed out. Everyone in the city was united in theory, but desperation led to people putting themselves first.

We were not allowed outside. The starvation and the hypothermic conditions had seen cannibalism become increasingly common in the city. Initially, people were hacking off limbs from the fresh corpses on the street. With thousands of people dying of starvation each day in the city, there was plenty of supply. It was understandable that many believed there was little alternative. The more disturbing occurrence was when those still living became targets.

More than 2,000 people were arrested in the city for cannibalism. If that is how many people were caught, you must know that far more people committed the offence and remained undetected. Those who ate from corpses were jailed. Those who took people still alive and killed them for their meat were executed. You cannot understand the desperation that drove people to such lengths. In some cases, parents killed one of their own children to feed the remainder of their family.

Before the rise of cannibalism, other animals were highly sought after. With so little food available for people, animals had little prospect of remaining adequately fed. Horses were dropping dead in the street, and people would gather to hack off meat or scoop out offal. People with pets they valued had to ensure they kept them closely watched and indoors, for outside, they would attract the attention of the desperate. When household situations were dire enough, the temptation of the loved family pets would become too much after burying other family members.

Our situation was less desperate than some. We had more stockpiles of various staples from the start of the Siege. It left us with very little, but it was still more than many had. Maybe, in a way, this helped make the decision to stay, which most would say had proven wrong.

The army created an ice road across Lake Lagoda to bring more supplies into the city. When the trucks turned around, they evacuated more people. As a family, we were not leaving. The ice road became known as The Road of Life. It helped our city survive but was far from a perfect plan. Many trucks broke through the ice and sank. The supplies that got through did not feed the masses, merely providing slight sustenance for the armed forces and little for anyone else.

We had burned furniture to provide heat. We'd had rations cut, with nothing being made available to those who didn't work. Aunt Yulia began working at the hospital, and although just twelve years old, Anastasia joined her. Between Mama and Yulia, they ensured she always had an escort to and from the hospital. With six of us in the house, we needed the additional rations to have any hope of survival.

One day, Mama had been out since early in the morning. The earlier you arrive, the further up the queue you were, maximising the chances of getting your full rations. Aunt Yulia had gone the previous day but got nothing, so we were desperate. As the hours passed, our concerns grew. Not only were we hungry, but whenever someone was out of the house, there was no certainty that they would return. That was the reality of life in the city through the Siege. As much as we looked forward to what they may bring home, what mattered most was to see them safe.

The initial assumption was that the line had been moving slowly. Eventually, Aunt Yulia suggested that she may have gone elsewhere if she could not get rations from the usual spot. As hours passed, the full range of worries started infiltrating our minds. While us children slept, Aunt Yulia and Babushka would have begun to panic.

Waking the following day without my mother seemed strange, yet there was no reason for overwhelming fear. As a child in the darkness of our basement, I never knew the time or the day, so I had no idea how long her food search should have taken nor how long it had been since she left.

Like my father four years earlier and my brothers the preceding year, my mother did not come home. There was never a time when the adults acknowledged that she was gone, but the past had taught me enough that you didn't wait to be told about tragedy, you felt it within.

Was she attacked after claiming her rations by someone at the ultimate point of desperation? Had she been left to slowly die in the snow, weakened by malnourishment and exposed to extreme conditions? Had the Nazis broken the line to be right outside our door? Had she been hit in a bombing attack? It did not matter. She was yet another victim of the Siege.

Aunt Yulia found her body several blocks from home. She had been shot. It appeared to have been motivated by theft, as our ration cards were not on her. Ration cards were the most valuable possession in the city. Not only had we lost Mama, but we had lost our individual claim for rations. While our ability to report this and get new cards would happen, it took time, which based on our resources, we did not have much of. When we got new cards, it would only be for five, having previously been surviving on eight ration cards for the six of us.

I can't remember how Babushka explained it to me. She knew that with just Yulia and her left to provide for three children, the chances of her meeting the same fate had grown significantly. At a moment when she should have been mourning the loss of her child, she was forced into the role of protecting her daughter's one surviving child. At the same time, I had to accept that my immediate family were all gone. A few people lose their four closest relatives by the age of eight, but if they do, you would suspect it was through one catastrophe. I had lost all four at different points. Mama was the only body ever witnessed and confirmed as deceased to us. In a scene of devastation like this city had been struck by, there was far too much death and horror even to identify who the corpses were on so many occasions and insufficient means to notify anyone. Knowing what had happened was unusual.

As winter passed, one less threat faced us, with the temperatures rising to a more survivable level. Bombings remained a constant, as did the prospect of malnutrition due to the small quantities of food we were made to live off. Bread rations had increased to 300 grams daily for us, and an additional supplement for Aunt Yulia and Anastasia due to their work at the local hospital. Anastasia was running errands for staff throughout the hospital. Babushka, Dasha and I would remain in the basement for what seemed like an eternity each day, praying they would return. The passing of the family after they left the cellar had left scars. Now, every time someone left, I doubted they would return. There seemed an heir of certainty that each of them would meet the same fate one day. If this happened, what hope would a 70-year-old, a 9-year-old and an 8-year-old possibly have?

Babushka spent the time singing songs, reading poems and telling us stories. In time, these all became so familiar that I'm sure I had a fiction catalogue that extended well beyond what most people ten times my age ever possessed. Dasha and I would smile at the stories and compete with new stories we'd create, but the smiles would invariably disappear at some point when the fantasy worlds we were making would skirt too close to the reality of the world right above us.

With exposure to the outside world, Aunt Yulia and Anastasia understood the extent of the problems far more. Anastasia was now part of a team of children helping to fight fires caused by the bombings. This was being done at night, making it impossible for her to continue the work she had been doing at the hospital. She said that Dasha and I should go and assist at the hospital, but Babushka couldn't accept this.

I remember her words so clearly. 'This war has taken my daughter, her husband, and my grandsons. I have no doubt it will soon take me, but I will not expose the two youngest. There is no reason to fight if nothing is left at the end. When we came down here, we knew that anything could happen, but I always said that starting from the youngest, everything would be done to protect our future. At any cost, I will ensure Ekaterina is safe. Beyond that, I will ensure that Dasha is safe at any cost. That is all that is left, as I had to let you take risks, my dear Anastasia, as much as it breaks my heart. If only the situation allowed, I would have you here with the other girls rather than exposing you to more risk above ground.' She said all this with tears streaming down her face. She had been such a tower of strength through all we'd endured, but there is a point for everyone where the emotion can no longer be hidden.

I don't know if my memory clouds the truth, but I seldom remember crying myself throughout these horrors. I had become so numb to all that had happened that it didn't seem like tragedy, just the natural way of the world.

Having just turned eight, I didn't understand that a twelve-year-old should not work in a war zone. Likewise, I didn't know that an eight-year-old shouldn't be exposed to this horror. I accepted that my actions should be to follow the orders issued by someone older. So long as Babushka said stay, I would do so. Anastasia seemed to resent all she was doing, while children just a little younger appeared to do nothing but drain our few precious resources. Dasha and I were both ready to do as we were told, but this was exactly what we were doing at that stage.

If only we could all have a decent meal and conquer this hunger, then the ability to cope with every other part of this horror could become manageable.

CHAPTER 11

January 2, 2022

ADAM

Dinner was provided for the tour group tonight at a downtown restaurant and wine bar called Wine Gogh. It was an excellent opportunity to catch up with everyone on our tour and discover what they did today so we could stockpile some good ideas for the remaining free time we would get in the city.

Not only were we treated to a great menu and wine list, but as the name suggested, there was a real Van Gogh theme to the décor. Reproductions of the Starry Night, the Church at Auvers, Night Café at Arles and more of the great artists' paintings adorned the walls. It isn't overdone and provides enough exposure to the great Dutch master's work to justify the theme. There isn't much to the food and drink that ties in with Van Gogh or even his Dutch heritage and French residency, but it all looks good. When you are only spending a week in a country, it makes more sense that the meals you eat are representative of that country's cuisine, so the fact that we had a predominantly Russian menu should not be a source of disappointment.

Louise and I were amongst the first to arrive and were enjoying a glass of Russian cabernet sauvignon when our most regular companions, English couple Harry and Judy, joined us. Their adult children, Ben and Nikki, were also on the tour but had spent the afternoon doing their own thing and were yet to turn up at Wine Gogh.

'You don't waste time,' Harry said, eyeing the wine.

'This is our eighth. We've been here since lunch,' I joked. Luckily, they knew my dry sense of humour enough by now not to take me seriously and asked what we had done through the day. I explained our trip to Pyshechnaya and the story of Ekaterina.

'That would have been brilliant,' Judy said. 'What you get from an official tour guide or a history book is always that sense of a standard story. You've gone behind the scenes and got something completely authentic. I'm jealous.'

'Louise was horrified that I brought her halfway around the world to spend our whole time in doughnut shops, but she understands why now. She's no longer so bothered by the idea.'

'Your approach to every city is to head straight for a bakery. This time you've just found a reason to justify it,' Louise said.

'If I can get away with it, I might keep trying it,' I said. 'What did you two do today?'

'We went out to Zenit Saint Petersburg's stadium and did a tour there in the morning,' Harry said.

'All part of our negotiations which led to the Faberge Museum just before coming here,' Judy added.

'Ah, we went there too,' Louise said.

'Stunning, wasn't it?' Judy said while I drifted off slightly to discuss the football stadium with Harry. We were then joined by Johannes and Marizane, a couple from Cape Town in South Africa who had just arrived. They always seemed out of step with the rest of the group, mainly regarding punctuality.

'Afrikaans time,' Marizane said as her excuse for being late. 'People move at their own pace back home. You always double-check when you have an appointment; do you mean 9 a.m. or 9 a.m. Afrikaans time? The latter means whenever you manage to get there. The 9 a.m. is just a rough estimate.'

They were a friendly couple but usually seemed happiest, keeping to themselves. Every time we got on the tour bus in Moscow, we would be waiting for the two of them to arrive before we could leave. They had skipped most of the optional extras on the tour, and I was surprised to see they joined us here, though this was paid for in our tour cost, so that may have been a factor.

'How was your day?' I asked, only to find that they'd spent most of the day at the hotel and just did a slow wander through the streets late in the afternoon.

Carol, an American in her mid-fifties travelling with her doctor son, came by and asked about our rendezvous with Ekaterina. We'd seen her at breakfast this morning and told her about our adventure there yesterday and that we were going back for the full story, so she was fascinated to hear how it had gone.

'That is travel at its absolute best,' she said. 'Forget the travel guides and the top ten tourist site lists. Find the most definitive example of the authentic city and go from there. I had a similar experience in Florence a couple of years ago. Missed everything I was intending to see, yet had a more memorable trip than anywhere I'd ever been.'

Our entrées came to the tables, and in reflection on the global nature of the wine list, I moved on to a South American pinot. We were all sharing plates of antipasto and bruschetta, all of which were enjoyable without being anything special. I was far more impressed when the mains came. I had veal cheek, which was beautiful, but the array of other options delivered to the table all looked equally appetising. Louise loved her salmon, Harry had cod, Judy had duck, and a couple of people had an exquisite-looking fillet mignon.

I'd been surprised they'd sent us somewhere so Western when showing off Russia, but it was a delicious meal. Food had not been a highlight of the Russian leg of our trip. While it felt awful speaking badly of food after hearing of hundreds of thousands of deaths from starvation, it often was a significant component of our times in different cities. In Russia, we had already experienced so many magical moments, but pyshki aside, food had been down the list. This meal had been something of a redemption.

Before anyone was ready for dessert, we mingled and got more ideas of what other highlights different people had found. Another English family was on the tour, and they had gone to Kronstadt, a settlement on an island in the middle of the Gulf of Finland that wasn't too far from tomorrow's destination of Peterhof Palace.

'We went ice skating,' Cherie said. A fellow Australian, Cherie was in her early twenties and had bonded closely with the rest of the under 30s on the trip, and a group of them had made the short trip across to New Holland Island, which was only a few blocks past the Mariinsky Theatre.

'Louise and I had practised ice skating back home to do it when we were here, but we've barely done any. We did once in Germany and then had a real quick skate in Gorky Park the other day.'

'They wouldn't call it skating, Adam,' Louise said. 'We put skates on and held on to the rail for dear life, barely moving.'

'There's another way?' I asked.

Cherie laughed. 'I'm hardly any better. Jeff and Jeremy, that's another story,' she said, referring to Carol's son Jeff and Canadian Jeremy, who probably learned to skate before they could walk.

I thought the best person to have asked about her day was Lila, our guide.

'I went and had lunch at my mum's house. Just a sandwich, a cup of coffee and a conversation. Life is different when you are in your hometown. I love showing the city's highlights and looking for the little features nobody knows about. My free time isn't spent in the Hermitage or Saint Isaacs.'

'Yeah, but you must be an encyclopedia of where the best places to eat and drink are.'

'No more than any local. I spend a lot of time in Moscow, so I know as many places there. When I am there, I don't have the option of staying home like I do here. I ended up constantly experiencing new things there. You travel a lot, right?'

I nodded.

'When you are home, you discover less than when you travel, don't you?

I continued to nod. 'At home, there are always favourite spots that demand regular returns, reducing the opportunities to try new places.'

'Exactly,' she said, which led to her acknowledging that she could recommend a few good places to eat if I felt I needed them through the week.

'So why doesn't the tour go to those places?

'I don't set the itinerary for your tour. The tour company engaged me to deliver the tour that they set up. We end up in places that are ideal for tourists. I go to places that are out of the way, look like nothing, but focus on good food at good prices.'

Among the others in the group, some explored the underground network, some focused on the parks and gardens, and others spent more time in the various museums. I was surprised that nobody else had referenced Pyshechnaya, not based on my love of the product but on the frequency with which it shows up on people's guides to the city.

'I wouldn't have swapped our experience for anyone's,' Louise said, finally acknowledging the uniqueness of our experience.

Our time in Russia was more than halfway through, yet it seemed like we'd only just arrived. That is the problem with travel. You watch the calendar slowly tick over as you count down the days until you leave. Then, when your trip begins, time moves at an utterly incomparable rate. Time normally goes faster as you get older, but when you are travelling, it doesn't matter what age you are. Time moves at an uncontrollably fast pace.

CHAPTER 12

March 1943

EKATERINA

They say that the older you get, the faster time goes. Stuck in a basement, freezing, hungry, having lost most of your loved ones and living in fear for your own life, time goes fast for nobody. For a child who already finds time moving slowly, the situation we found ourselves in meant the movement of time was torturous. It seemed an enemy despite the fact we tried to shut ourselves from it. What is the point of times and dates when you had nothing to look forward to? Mealtime did not exist. Sleep was whenever you could. You may drift off when you were weak enough, and nobody knew if you would ever wake again. While we cared if others did, nobody cared too much if they didn't themselves.

Even Yulia and Anastasia didn't need to know about times for work. They had no particular time to be at the hospital. They arrived when they could. They worked as long as they could. In this city, the hospitals couldn't manage the dying and the sick. All that could be done was to delay the inevitable. All anybody could be asked for was their best.

Hospitals were largely irrelevant. People dropped dead in the streets. People passing them barely noticed, being half-dead themselves. People felt despair when these scenes became commonplace a year earlier, but now they were immune to it. Beyond the dangers, Babushka wanted to protect us from what we would see. It was futile though, for as time passed, it became apparent that we'd have to face it eventually.

As time passed, Yulia and Anastasia were not home as often. They had greater security over their rations at the hospital and were often able to get additional scraps to feed them while there. They would come home with rations for Babushka and us two girls, sleep, and then return to the hospital. I envied this. We were prisoners in the basement. In another way, they were prisoners, but each day offered them a degree of difference that we did not have.

Babushka began playing a game with us when it came time to share a piece of bread.

'Close your eyes. I want you to think about the plate in front of you. Imagine having any food in the world in front of you and on that plate. On my plate, I have got a beef stroganoff. Beautifully cooked beef strips in a creamy sauce with mushrooms and potatoes.'

She put a tiny piece of bread in her mouth, but her mind contemplated the combination of flavours she had just explained. We didn't see how there was any point to this, but we indulged her. Besides, she seemed to be making her bread last longer this way, and the smile on her face was far greater than what we were used to seeing from her or anyone else.

'What are you eating tonight, Dasha?'

'I have got Pirozhki,' she said. 'The pastry is much nicer than just bread and wrapping around meat, cabbage, and cheese. That is what I shall have.' She copied Babushka and slowly let the bread dissolve in her mouth.

'So is this what our first meals will be when the war is over, Babushka,' I asked.

'When the war is over, we can eat these things whenever we want,' she said.

'Alright, on my plate is pyshki,' I said.

'That's not much of a dinner,' Babushka said.

'Look at my plate. That is all I have. The dough has been fried, and they have been coated with icing sugar. It is perfect.'

I broke my bread section into four and consumed them one by one. With each little piece I put in my mouth, I talked of another pyshki.

'Well, why not, I suppose. I will come and have pyshki with you when the war is over.'

Anastasia arrived home distressed, yelling as she ran in the door.

'What is it?'

'A man tried to take me. He grabbed me but was too weak to hang on when I started punching and kicking. Then he tried to run after me, so I ran like I hadn't run for a long time. I don't think anyone was going to help me.'

There is a phrase I have heard people use: 'I couldn't care less.' It means they don't care. Couldn't care is what applied here during the Siege. The people physically couldn't bring themselves to care about what happened in their line of sight. If someone was mistreated, so be it. Everyone here was a victim in one way or another. Nobody would condone an adult attacking a child, but stopping it became too difficult.

'Why is your mother not with you?' Babushka asked.

'Too much to do. She sent me home to sleep and bring your rations. See if these two are ready to earn their keep while the rest of the family puts their lives on the lines for them.'

'I have been willing to do anything, anytime,' Dasha said. She refused to be looked down on by her sister. 'Babushka, when you allow it, I will work anywhere I can to serve my family, city and country.'

Babushka put her head into her hands, refusing to discuss the matter. She looked at all possibilities towards the end of the conflict. If we were to be conquered, then any choice she made for us now was irrelevant, and our fate would be sealed. If we were to win the battle, then keeping the children safe was what she considered paramount. She had always taken the approach that the protection in the family worked from the youngest up. She didn't want Anastasia to risk being out, but it had been necessary once the boys and my Mama were gone.

'Do you want to stop going to the hospital?'

'No. I am proud that I am part of the solution,' she said before looking around at Dasha and me and continuing. 'Rather than part of the problem.'

'We will discuss this at some point with your mother. Until we agree to make changes, everything remains the same. Understood.'

It was the strongest and sternest I had heard Babushka since we had been confined to the basement. It may have looked to be directed principally at Dasha, but I knew it was meant more towards Anastasia. To say that her life could be risked when ours were being protected would be disturbing to hear, so it wouldn't be said. The consequences would remain, the reasoning could be easily interpreted, but the words would forever remain unsaid.

Yulia had still not returned by morning. However busy it had been, there was only so long someone could work, and we all became worried.

'Leave it. I will find her,' Anastasia insisted.

She was gone for most of the day. She had worked a shift at the hospital before returning, able to tell us that her mother was now a patient in the hospital where she had been working as a nurse.

'She is very ill. There has been an outbreak of disease, and they haven't let me in to see her. They want to avoid further spreading, but there is much of this. Dead bodies in the street. Rats are now the plentiful living creatures in our city. First, it was the starvation, then the cold; now it is the disease. I don't understand why they ever needed to drop a bomb.'

Anastasia broke down, one of the rare times through all of the pain we lived through that someone did that in front of the rest of us. Behaviour is predominantly learned, and we'd all learned to keep it in. A part of us sometimes overpowers how we've learned to deal with certain scenarios. For Anastasia, this was one.

Anastasia returned to the hospital each day and said her final goodbye within a week. Aunt Yulia was dead. Another member of our family. Another cause. The same result.

If there was a small source of solace at the time, it is that Yulia had a more dignified burial than anyone else in the family. Dying in the hospital, there was someone to deal with it. Dying with disease, there was a definite need to deal with it quickly as well.

Anastasia barely spoke to us from this point on. She refused to collect rations for anyone else, so Babushka began to take us outside, and we went with her to collect them. Unlike a year earlier, the rations were consistently available. More supplies had come since the Road of Life was established across Lake Lagoda. Probably more relevant was that significantly fewer people were left to collect rations between the million people who had fled the city and the hundreds of thousands already dead. Our provisions remained meagre, but they were reliable.

A few weeks later, Anastasia didn't return home. Despite the divide in the house, it became another crisis we had to endure. We asked at the hospital, but they had not seen her for several days. We searched the area. Nobody was able to provide any information. Multiple people knew who we were talking about, but none knew her whereabouts. In the middle of the war, there was minimal opportunity to find one who was lost. Unlike the early stages of the Siege, corpses were now being collected fast, but they were not always identified. When we found the city's burial team, they could not tell us of any young girl of fourteen that they'd collected and buried from this area in recent days.

There was no escape from the city at this point. Winter over, the Road of Life would have closed. Perhaps she did attempt that escape, and maybe there were still trucks making it across, but it was always dangerous, and the later in the season it got, the more perilous the prospects. Over a thousand trucks and several thousand people were lost on the lake during the Siege. It was an escape route, but a hazardous and flawed one.

We never knew Anastasia's fate. Dead or alive, she was gone to us.

CHAPTER 13

January 3, 2022

ADAM

Straight after breakfast, we were on the bus with our tour group for a trek outside the city centre to visit the two grandest imperial palaces.

It took around half an hour on the bus before we arrived in Pushkin City. Along the journey, Lila gave us a lot of history about the palace and its connection to Russian history, so I felt like an authority before we arrived. The palace is not named after Catherine the Great, but Catherine the First, wife of Peter the Great. It began its construction during the reign of their daughter Elizabeth, and she is said to have chosen the blue exterior as a tribute to the colour of her mother's eyes.

'They liked their greats,' Louise said.

'Only Peter and Catherine,' I said. 'Though I guess anyone with the title 'Great' bestowed on them is also likelier to have more tributes around the country than anyone else. It can seem like everyone is Great, even if it is just two of them.'

We were let out a couple of hundred metres from the palace and first shown a statue of Alexander Pushkin. For the second time in a couple of hours, we were paying tribute to a man whose name was indelibly familiar to me yet whose work I didn't know. The town is now called Pushkin in his honour. Originally, it was called Tsarskoye Selo, meaning the village of the tsars.

For 200 years, the palace was the summer home of the tsars of Russia. The original house was a nondescript home that naturally was upgraded multiple times before being considered worthy of such aristocracy. What had started as a wooden building would eventually become a palace with a circumference of nearly a kilometre. Size wasn't all it had going for it, with more than 100kg of gold being used to decorate the exteriors.

Getting inside proved to be far more of a challenge than Lila had suggested. The first stop was the cloakroom, where we had to leave our bags and jackets. This process took nearly twenty minutes and seemed the furthest thing from typical Russian efficiency. Things had been similar at the ballet last night, so perhaps it is the one aspect of life Saint Petersburg has struggled to come to terms with.

Our tour began with the Golden Enfilade of state rooms. We started on the State Staircase, the grandeur of its bannisters and reclining marble cupids preparing us for the visual treats to come. After working through several small but impressive rooms, we entered the Great Hall, or the Hall of Light as it is also known. It was a massive room covering the entire width of the palace, with nothing in the middle, making the space seem even greater. Well, not quite nothing was in the middle of the room. There were hundreds of people in the room with us. We had about twenty people on our tour, but our group was one of many here.

Not only was the opulence of the room decoration spectacular, but the views on both sides highlighted how special the park grounds were.

'Remember the Palace of Versailles?' I asked Louise rhetorically. 'I think this place is more spectacular.' Whether this assessment was skewed through recency bias was hard to say. Whatever was freshest in the mind always seemed comparatively more memorable, but ranking the palace so highly wasn't purely based on this. Along with the gold surrounding the room, the ceiling itself was reminiscent of the Sistine Chapel, with its elaborate work above us called 'The Triumph of Russia,' which is undoubtedly one of the most significant works of its type anywhere.

After roughly ten minutes in the ballroom, we moved onwards, slowly as it was, forced to be on account of the volume of people touring the palace. The next highlight was the White Dining Room, a small but no less opulent place for more casual meals.

'Yeah, breakfast in here, lunch in the Green Dining Room, then dinner in....well, I'm sure we're about to find another one soon,' Harry said.

'Must've been a hard life,' I replied.

'They didn't mind looking at themselves,' Judy added as we walked into the portrait hall, featuring giant portraits of both Catherine and Elizabeth, far from the only paintings of them within the palace.

Next, was the highlight of the palace, the Amber Room. Some have referred to this as the eighth wonder of the world. While I've heard of at least ten different places to have been called that, it is undoubtedly a wonder. It was designed and constructed in Prussia and was initially planned to occupy part of a palace in Berlin. The Prussian monarch gifted it to Peter the Great, who had it installed in the Catherine Palace.

The room is priceless. More than six tonnes of amber were used in the room, meaning the room was of unparalleled value on raw materials alone. What the finished product became, crafted so superbly, pushed this to another level again. It was indisputably one of the greatest triumphs of art and craft ever created.

Lila explained the later history of the room:

'When the Germans had begun their march towards Saint Petersburg, experts were assigned to remove all the treasures from the city. They could not move the amber from this room and tried to hide it by covering the room with wallpaper. Such a plan was destined to fail as the Germans were aware of its existence. Their soldiers were able to remove all the amber over a few days and moved it to Konigsberg Castle in Prussia. The mystery began when that city was under attack at the end of World War II. Some say it was destroyed in the conflict, as the British Air Force heavily bombed Konigsberg Castle. The Red Army then advanced on the town and took the castle. Many people state that the Amber Room had already been deconstructed and sent onward before this time. It was never found again, either reconstructed or dismantled and redistributed, so the truth of its fate remains a mystery today.'

The room was never seen after the Second World War. It may have ended up in the possession of a wealthy oligarch who kept it hidden away forever. It was more likely destroyed by the Red Army, with the government unwilling ever to reveal that they had destroyed their greatest treasure. Other theories include the idea that Stalin had the original Amber Room replaced by a replica which is all that the Nazis originally stole, the original being hidden somewhere in Russia. It seems impossible that we will ever know the true fate of the original Amber Room. Whether it survived the war's end is largely irrelevant if the world would never see it again anyway.

'Like Anastasia,' Louise whispered to me. Initially, I shot a puzzled look at her before realising she was referring to Ekaterina's cousin.

Lila explained that the room we were now looking at had been reconstructed panel by panel by master artisans.

'It took 24 years to complete. Experts from here and in Germany used black and white photographs and original blueprints to reconstruct the room exactly as it had stood before 1941. Given how hard it was to find modern craftsmen who knew about carving amber, it was a miracle that this could ever be recreated.'

'So this isn't quite the same priceless historic relic,' Johannes asked.

'Perhaps not, but it is genuine amber. The construction cost was tens of millions of dollars, and the work involved in building it was more complex and a greater achievement than the original. It may not be the original, but it is effectively priceless.'

Coming to the end of the tour, we walked down a corridor with an exhibition of photographs highlighting the atrocities the city and this palace endured during the Siege of Leningrad in the early 1940s. It is easy to appreciate the beauty throughout this city, but understanding all that underpins it is when the beauty truly begins to matter.

Among the photos, I saw children from the start of the 1940s, and I immediately thought of Ekaterina and her family.

'Hearing the stories directly from her brought a whole other perspective, but now seeing the pictures adds further weight to the stories. That is how young she'd have been when the Siege started. To live through those experiences at that age.' I shook my head at the thought of it.

'Thinking about your doughnut woman?' Carol asked.

I nodded. I could tell from her tone that she didn't understand. Every story has light and dark; she'd only taken the light. Considering the enormity of what was in front of us in these pictures, it didn't require hearing Ekaterina's version of events to know just how much pain was involved.

'Do you think that would validate a devotion through life to doughnuts?' Carol asked.

'I think it would explain why she isn't like the average person we would know of that age. Any person becomes who they are through the sum of everything they've been through. When you've lived through history's greatest tragedy, you're somewhat destined to be slightly different to the average senior citizen when you reach that age.'

'Wouldn't she be more like the average in this city, though?'

'Not exactly. Very few people stayed here throughout the Siege, and most children who did, and survived, didn't lose everyone and get left to their own devices at such a young age.'

We left the palace to see a little of the grounds. Catherine Park extends so far that a full day would not be enough to see everything, but the remaining twenty minutes we were left with wouldn't even allow us a proper overview. There were the immaculate grounds, the Cameron Gallery, the Alexander Palace, the Chinese Theatre, and the White Tower, just to name a few. The highlight for us was seeing the length of the line and knowing that if we'd made our own way here at this point, rather than two hours at the Catherine Palace, we'd have spent two hours in the line alone. I thought Pyshechnaya had a long line on our first visit, but this was unbelievable.

Louise and I wandered towards the large lake near the park's centre. An island in the middle housed a hall used as a private concert venue for the estate's custodians. This was a hall on an island on a lake. It's all just part of the backyard of the summer house for the tsars. If that was not luxury, then indeed nothing was.

In summer, boats take people out to look at the small island. Unlike the waters of the rivers and canals downtown, the small lake here was frozen over. It didn't look solid enough to be moving across, so it seemed impossible to imagine how heavy trucks could have ever driven across a frozen lake.

CHAPTER 14

December 1943

EKATERINA

Before the third winter of the Siege, a land corridor had been established along the coast of Lake Lagoda. Through this, there was a way in and out of the city, and although conditions were still dangerous, the situation was better than we'd faced the previous two years. The impact of that time had been severe on us. Dasha and I were on the verge of malnutrition. Babushka had always focussed on ensuring our well-being over hers, and the impact of this was now taking its toll. She was gravely ill.

Throughout the Siege, the intention had been to keep Dasha and me as safe as possible by staying indoors. This was no longer possible. All collection of rations had to be done by the two of us. We always went together, conscious of the risks that we faced. The vulnerability that existed when alone was far more significant. We had heard many stories of children going outside and never returning. Nobody had the strength to resist most threats at this time, but few people had the power to issue them anymore. It was not uncommon for people to be friendly and invite us to come with them, but we were always suspicious of their intentions. We were never threatened in any aggressive way, but it was the honey trap that was most frequently used to steal children. Whenever someone offered us a meal, we understood the genuine prospect of us being the meal.

With temperatures in the minus twenties, we came home one day with our rations to find Babushka sleeping. Perhaps we both knew immediately that she wasn't sleeping, but we couldn't accept it. She was little more than a skeleton, the little exposed flesh blue from the cold.

Walking to get rations, we saw corpses in the street every day. We saw them fresh, after time had passed, and when rats had started feasting on them. In best-case scenarios, these were buried in mass graves, but there was a reliance on someone getting them to one. What could we do with Babushka's body?

I was not quite ten, and Dasha was just a year older. Although Babushka weighed so little, our strength had been so compromised through the Siege that we could not lift her. Although we had left her body there for the first day, we knew we couldn't keep her in the basement with us any longer. We started to roll her corpse across the room, pushing towards the stairs. From there, we began the slow process of dragging the body up the stairs before we heard the sound of the air raid siren.

German bombings had not stopped. If anything, they were becoming more prevalent. The Red Army had pushed the Nazis back on a couple of fronts, so there was a level of promise that the Siege may come to an end soon. If they were to fail, the Nazis were determined to damage and take what they could. Looting and destruction of landmarks became widespread. Bombings were conducted less as a strategy for conquering and more as a way to create free rein for them to take the wealth they sought. Mostly, this centred around specific parts of the city, with less focus on suburbs like ours, but we were still far from being safe.

Dasha and I continued pulling the corpse up the stairs the following day. The war mentally broke us, so this task's emotional impact was much easier than you'd imagine. After a full day's work, we got her upstairs, and then we got her outside more easily. We rolled her out to the street, hoping the authorities would find her and take her to an appropriate grave. In such circumstances, there was no disrespect in not performing a proper burial, for such events had ceased to occur in the city through the Siege. We couldn't notify anyone else that she'd died. If the authorities knew that it was just us two children, we would be taken, possibly separated, and raised by a state institution. We were determined that after all we'd survived, we would continue to make our way on our own, however hard that would be.

As we returned to the basement, the closest thing to a funeral for Babushka played out. This was merely Dasha and I talking about her and how she would always sacrifice anything for us. We must never forget her and everything she was to us.

We agreed that it was now up to us to carry on her legacy and the legacies of our family. We were to stick together through anything life threw at us. We were to remember everything about our departed family members, whatever came our way. Life, however cruel, had delivered these circumstances to us. We had the responsibility of moving forward in the best way possible.

A couple of weeks later, it was my tenth birthday, though we didn't know when it came and went. It was just another day of survival: another day of going out together to collect our rations, another day of avoiding other people, and another day of answering as few questions as possible about why our parents were not collecting the family's rations. We explained that Babushka was unwell but said nothing further.

We kept hoping to find Anastasia. We always considered that she just wanted to run away from us. With Babushka gone, she would now be able to make the decisions of the house. We wanted her back, though we knew that among all the options, the most likely was that she had left the city or that she had left this life. We could only hope that the loss of her mother had prompted her to take the first of those options and that she had managed to do so safely.

On January 27th, 1944, the Siege of Leningrad was officially over. The German forces on the city's southern outskirts had been expelled, and freedom was returned to the city. The remaining population was small and shell-shocked, but the recovery could slowly begin. The threats would take time to disappear, for the most severe dangers we had faced came from each other and from nature rather than the enemy, but it was the enemy's actions that had caused this. With them defeated, we could work together on re-establishing life in our city.

By the end of the Siege, about a million people had died, roughly five times the loss of life that would later be experienced in the atomic bombs of Hiroshima and Nagasaki combined. I don't wish to diminish any horror by making another seem worse, but no city endured anything like we experienced. Our city began the war with a population of three million. It ended the Siege with less than half a million, the numbers only beginning to return after the end of the war.

Less than 3% of these deaths came from bombs and shelling. Nearly all of the deaths were from the impact of the blockade. Starvation, hypothermia and disease.

I began the war with seven relatives and finished with five dead and one unknown. It is horrific but also comparatively standard.

The job required to rebuild the city was enormous, and the job required to rebuild individuals' lives was even greater.

The last footprint of the Nazis was in the places they had occupied south of the city. The Catherine and Peterhof Palaces had been home to them throughout the Siege. The Amber Room had been deconstructed and sent to Germany, never to be found again. As their final departure point, they left Peterhof Palace burning and returned to Germany, defeated but having taken everything they could ransack from our city.

CHAPTER 15

January 3, 2022

ADAM

A forty-kilometre drive through southern Saint Petersburg took us from the Catherine Palace to Peterhof Palace. Peterhof was inspired by Peter the Great's visit to the Palace of Versailles just outside of Paris. He was so taken with the French estate that he wanted an equivalent, and to this end, he engaged architects and landscapers who would deliver a similar result.

Peterhof is sometimes referred to as the world capital of fountains. The Grand Cascade alone, which runs from the northern façade of the Grand Palace to the Marine Canal, comprises sixty-four separate fountains and more than two hundred bronze statues.

The main palace building here is a very similar-looking structure to the Catherine Palace, both built in a similar style with many of the same architects involved in each design. While both could be classified as Baroque style, they both possess a unique Saint Petersburg appearance and would look out of place anywhere else. While the Catherine Palace's distinctive sky-blue colouring stands out against the golden surrounds more than the yellow dominant colouring at Peterhof, the allure here is greatest with the view from the sea's edge. For some, this is the point of arrival and undoubtedly would be the ideal way to make your way here.

The German Army occupied the palace between 1941 and 1944. When the Germans first invaded the Soviet Union, preparations were made to protect the treasures at Peterhof. Still, only a small portion of the palace's most valuable items could be protected. Peterhof was heavily damaged near the end of this time, with many of the fountains destroyed. The Germans left the palace burning as they evacuated, and the rebuilding process began and continued for the best part of thirty years. Peterhof was renamed Petrodvorets at the end of the war to avoid having a German-sounding name, but like the city itself, it reverted to its previous name in the post-Soviet era.

Although the palace appeared enormous at first view, it is comparatively moderate in size, long but narrow. What it lacked in size, it made up for in majesty within its thirty rooms. The ballroom glistened with such golden features that I felt sunglasses would have been appropriate. It almost outdazzled the Catherine Palace's Amber Room, even if it was less significant. There was the throne room, a massive area set aside for a throne against the far wall and open space beyond with nothing more than views onto the gulf. True to its name, the portrait hall had every spare inch of wall taken with portraits of every prominent Romanov.

A further example of the inspiration Peter the Great had taken from his visit to Paris and Versailles was the Marly Palace, situated in the western half of the Lower Park. It was named after a lodge of Louis XIV at Marly le Roi, which Peter had visited in 1717, and he liked the idea of a more understated, personal sanctuary.

Two ponds surround Marly Palace and can only be reached by crossing one of three little footbridges across the crescent-shaped pond. The whole section is covered sufficiently with trees that the palace itself is hidden, which is the sanctity Peter wanted. This highlights the difference to most of the imperial residences. Having become so accustomed to looking at buildings that commanded attention, the Marly Palace was the equivalent of a wallflower seeking to hide from prying eyes. That said, it was still a beautiful building, opulent beyond what most people would ever hope to find in a home. It is a simple square structure that provides comfort and serenity, particularly amongst the beauty of its surroundings.

'Imagine the wealth to have this as your house, let alone your little spare tenth house,' Louise said.

'At least in Peter's time,' I explained, 'the Russians, as a whole, were doing well enough that there weren't significant issues with this use of wealth. You can understand how a revolution was guaranteed when poverty was everywhere while all this wealth existed.

The Marly Palace was in the lower gardens, and we made our way through this area but were told we had to speed up. One of the features was the choreographed fountain show closer to the main palace. Fountains were not confined to that area of the estate, and as we made our way, we encountered several impressive fountains that connected with my memories of Versailles.

The Grand Cascade fountain show draws parallels with famous similar presentations at the Bellagio in Las Vegas or by the Burj Khalifa in Dubai. Water shoots out of a golden sculpture and is choreographed to music as it pours down the hillside in a feast for the senses.

Experiences of every different type shape us. Possibly through seeing the same kind of shows in other locations, we were less excited by this one than most people nearby. It was well worth seeing, but on its own, nothing unique.

'Shit!'

The next fountain wasn't quite so entertaining for me, but the rest of our group found it brilliant. The joke fountain sits amongst oak trees and sprays passers-by who inadvertently activate it by stepping on a particular stone. Generally, as I lurked at the back of the pack, I would have been safe. I paid the price after moving from the Grand Cascade quicker than most. It was cold enough that I didn't really appreciate the drenching, though, of course, in such weather, I was dressed in enough layers, with waterproofs on top, that it wasn't an issue.

'I thought you only moved that fast for beer,' Harry said.

'And doughnuts, cake, burgers, food in general,' Louise said.

'I'd try and defend myself, but there may be a little too much truth in all of that,' I said, accepting my weaknesses, if that's what they were going to be called, though I saw nothing wrong in showing my appreciation for the things I liked. I wasn't going to add the mystery fountain to that list.

We passed several other spectacular fountain displays, ranging from the giant Menager Fountain to the Chess Hill cascade with a centrepiece resembling a chessboard.

We worked our way down to the gulf, this time further along to find Monplaisir, the original palace on the site that Peter preferred. Apparently, Peter himself designed it.

'Did he have a palace for each week of the year?' I asked Lila.

'Nothing is ever perfect,' she said. 'The only way you can avoid having a house that is large enough for everything you want is to have a house so large that it will be too big to get around easily. When your capacity is unlimited, the best way to avoid such dilemmas is to have so many houses that you can accommodate every possible set of requirements. This particular place was his summer retreat.'

'I thought the Summer Palace was downtown,' I said.

'Yes. He had a Summer Palace and a Summer Retreat.'

I raised my eyebrows and shook my head before thinking that a $100 million lotto victory was all that stood in the way of me having something similar. Even that sum would be a drop in the ocean in comparative terms with the wealth the imperial family held.

What earned Peter the title great? He expanded the Russian Empire into one of Europe's great powers. Doing this through war, I'm sure the armies he defeated were not convinced of his greatness. The title was less about war victories or the accumulation of such impeccable residential property but for the positives he brought his people. Anywhere in the world, people seek the best results for themselves. They generally want the best for others, but their own wellbeing is the primary way they view the world. Peter's adoption of the principles stemming from the Enlightenment delivered a better life to his subjects, or a large enough proportion to be a hero. When Lenin led the overthrow of much of what Peter had created, he, too, became a hero respected throughout history.

When the Germans set fire as they retreated from Peterhof, the last place they left in Leningrad, the war had turned. The following year, the war was over. The Soviet Union led the Allies to victory. Stalin, far from alone, was victorious. For all of the atrocities he committed, he'd have been a hero through history among his people if only they had gained the benefit. The people continued to suffer, and Stalin's legacy became his failings, not his successes.

The people of Leningrad took generations to rebuild and recover. Before people had homes, the Imperial Palaces were being rebuilt, the symbolism being considered more important than the realities of the masses. Stalin saw his legacy threatened much like citizens had seen their lives threatened in the lead-up to this time.

Truth was noble. It was an ideal, but there were times when ideals had to be cast aside for greater priorities. In World War II, survival was paramount in Leningrad, and this was done via any means possible.

CHAPTER 16

December 1944

EKATERINA

'Dad, quick, get your gun,' Dasha screamed. 'Ekaterina is being attacked.'

The attacker panicked at the prospect of imminent gunfire and immediately got off me and ran to the door at top speed. He didn't wait for any validation of the threat. When the stakes are high enough, you don't analyse. You act. Immediately.

Nobody would believe that a pair of pre-teenage girls occupied this house alone. By screaming out to an adult male relative, the assumption would naturally be that such a person existed. The attacker was not much older than us, probably in his mid-teens. Most people who had evacuated the city were yet to return, so he likely was another survivor. He may have been too young to have worked with my brothers at the start of the Siege, but maybe he had done similar work by the end of it. Perhaps he thought it was time to collect his pay, taking what he wanted from anyone. It didn't matter what those people had already lost.

A community so united through tragedy should be too connected for such incidents to occur. Human nature extends beyond ideals. The city may celebrate its unity, but the individual's wants can corrupt these ideals. It may be a minority, but some will always see that the benefit to themselves justifies any action.

We couldn't speak to the police about the incident, for this would bring our living arrangements to our attention, and we would be made wards of the state. Dasha and I may not have been able to look after ourselves by anyone else's standards, but we were determined to remain as we were. If we could endure all we had, surviving this long, we believed we could do anything. I was battered and bruised, I was traumatised, and I was scared. Despite this, I continued to think that changing our current arrangements would only heighten the risks and fears we would be exposed to. We made that commitment to each other, and we were not going to do anything to sacrifice that at this point.

'What if he returns when he realises nobody else is here?'

'There may be no dad, but there is a gun. I am ready to use it,' Dasha said.

I had never been aware of a gun in the house, but Babushka had given Dasha instructions before she died. This tradition had been passed on ever since our fathers had left, with a new house leader responsible for keeping the rest of us safe. That we now had a twelve-year-old girl in charge was something that Papa and Uncle Dmitri could never have envisaged.

This city's traumas led to some examples of the best of humanity. Unfortunately, significantly more examples of the worst of humanity were displayed for each. If the Siege itself had not shown how evil and wrong life can be, then the actions of some of our people towards each other truly defined it. Cannibalism, child rape, murder. These weren't rare instances but standard occurrences.

You might think it was immoral for people to do such things. How can you tell a person anything is wrong when they have endured what the people here have experienced? Imagine the horror that someone must feel when committing to eating human flesh. That isn't something someone chooses. It is something that someone accepts as a final resort. The more final resorts someone faces, the more they lose all ability to make reasonable choices. Once they have lost virtually everything, they feel nothing is left to lose.

Like many in this city, the boy who attacked me had probably reached a point of having nothing left. By this stage, there is no right or wrong. Life is whatever you can get away with taking. What was he left with? Poverty, loneliness, virtually nothing. I don't want to sound sympathetic to my attacker, for that was not the case, but it is always best to try and understand why things happen, not just expect better.

The attacker had been an unmistakable signal to me that we shouldn't stay alone in the house. We weren't equipped to deal with significant issues that arose like this, however successful Dasha had been in driving him out. She may be prepared to shoot as necessary, but that was not a solution to any issue that arose.

'Life is cheap. You know that as well as I do. If someone steps in our way, I see no problem finishing them. The innocent people of this city have copped that non-stop in recent years, so there should be little issue with the same fate meeting the guilty,' she said.

'Dealing with intruders is just one of the issues,' I said. 'What will we do for food, clothing, heating, education, money?'

'Either we make do or throw ourselves at the authorities and end up in an orphanage. And you know what happens in orphanages?'

I didn't, and despite her going into detail about an array of horrors, I still couldn't be sure that this wasn't her way of scaring me into agreement. Dasha was adamant that however ill-equipped we were to survive on our own, our prospects remained best with our fate in our own hands.

'We have each other and whatever else, it is better to have someone you can trust. We're in it together, so as long as it is just the two of us, we can and will find a way,' she said.

We retained valid ration cards and went together to claim what we were entitled to. It was essential in our minds to avoid being alone, so we always went together. Although the siege had ended, the war continued, and there remained little prospect of finding much else across the city to add to our ability to get on. Our focus was simple: to stay safe at home and have enough to eat. Everything else was a future concern.

Although I had only experienced a very brief bit of schooling before the Siege, Babushka had effectively been my schoolteacher for several years. While the days of having a dedicated teacher had passed, we still had books in the house, and I began reading everything I could to keep educating myself. While we had desperate needs for anything that could be used to fuel fires, Babushka and Mum insisted on how critical books were, and they were spared as essential items. Now, even if we were reading material that we'd already read several times or were reading books unsuitable for children of our age, there were lessons in every text. We were keen to learn as much as possible. Pushkin, Dostoevsky, Tolstoy, Chekhov; it was hardly the material for a ten-year-old girl, but I hadn't lived the life of a ten-year-old girl, so why couldn't my understanding stretch a little further and more profoundly than usual?

Babushka had a couple of books she valued highly that expressed her love for some of the iconic parts of this city. She had a book that detailed all of the works on display in the Hermitage, and I couldn't wait for the day when I would be able to go and visit the museum and see the works referred to in this book. Another was a book on the history of the Kirov Ballet. We were taken to see a ballet before the Siege, but I was too young to recollect anything about it. I don't know how or when, but after reading about it repeatedly, I will see the Kirov Ballet.

CHAPTER 17

January 3, 2022

ADAM

'It isn't my thing,' I said, explaining my relative lack of enthusiasm to Lila about the evening ahead. It had been a long day visiting the two imperial palaces. On our way now to the ballet, my main focus for the evening was making sure I didn't embarrass anyone by falling asleep in the auditorium.

'I am not into football, but I still got swept up in the atmosphere when we hosted the World Cup. Anything big enough is easy to get caught in the event's magnitude. You don't need to be a purist, Adam. Even if you don't get great entertainment from the performance, a real traveller like you should appreciate the concept of being at the global home of any pursuit.'

My ignorance of ballet meant that the Mariinsky Theatre had meant nothing to me, though one of Lila's tidbits on the way there changed my mindset. As with the city, the theatre had changed names in the post-Soviet era. I immediately considered this a more significant event when I was informed that we would be attending the Kirov Ballet.

The Kirov name stemmed from the Bolshevik Sergei Kirov, whose assassination led to the Great Purge. Before the Russian Revolution, the Mariinsky Theatre had been its name, and the name returned in 1992, honouring the Empress Maria Alexandrovna, the wife of Alexander II.

'We are going to see The Nutcracker,' Lila said. 'You can't tell me you've never heard of it.'

'Yes, it and Swan Lake are probably the only two ballets I have heard of, but although I know the names, I know nothing else about them.'

'Both well over a century old,' she said. 'Both were composed by Tchaikovsky. Both were first performed right here at the Mariinsky Theatre. You're not coming along to watch a few people do some ballet. You're stepping into a theatre of world significance and seeing a performance of one of the high points of this art form in the very location where it was first done. That's living history, Adam.'

'Ok, I'm sold,' I said. I still didn't anticipate my ideal night, but it would be good to reflect on it and say I'd experienced it. I had considered getting tickets for the Bolshoi in Moscow, an equally famous theatre and company, but we'd run out of time, so conceding here was not a significant sacrifice for me.

From the outside, the theatre was typical of Saint Petersburg architecture, blending into the city's skyline rather than standing out the way that the opera houses of Sydney, Paris, Vienna and Milan all do. Inside, the Marinsky was a beautiful theatre with a layout that appeared far more audience-friendly than most I'd ever been in. The five tiers of the auditorium stretched for just a few rows each so that all audience members were close. The most impressive section was the Emperor's Box, a section of roughly thirty seats that would never have been filled as the elite classes would have ensured they were spaced out in the best seats in the house. They were elevated but central and still close to the main stage.

The Nutcracker is set at Christmas. As a result, it has been the most typically performed Christmas-time ballet worldwide ever since. Once, as a child, I had been to see my sister perform in a ballet school production, and I think it may have been The Nutcracker, but it was far enough back that I wasn't considering this to be my second time seeing the show.

It probably isn't worth saying too much about the story, as I was told that everyone knows it. I am not so sure about that. A little girl named Clara receives a nutcracker as a Christmas present. When Clara is attacked by a room full of giant mice, the nutcracker leads an army of toy soldiers to defeat them. The Nutcracker comes to life as a handsome prince. He travels with Clara across the Lemonade Sea, where they are greeted by the Sugarplum Fairy and are entertained by several performances from the inhabitants of her kingdom. Clara soon falls asleep before waking to find the nutcracker, a doll once again.

'Well?' Lila said when I first saw her outside the auditorium.

'Have you gone to the football since the World Cup?' She looked at me strangely, and I clarified my point by saying that I didn't expect to be headed back to the ballet anytime soon.

'Don't get me wrong, I admire the artistry and the athleticism. I'm happy that I got to experience the history of this venue. Though it isn't my thing, the music is still significant because, without realising it beforehand, I did know quite a bit of it.'

'It sounds like you did appreciate it then,' she said.

'He stayed awake,' Louise added.

'Like I say, it was worthwhile, but I wouldn't want to see it again. See, unlike the football, you can be pretty confident the result will be the same every time you go.'

'It is a performance, yes. You read a book or watch a movie, and they don't end differently each time,' Lila said.

'Yes, but generally, you read different books. People keep seeing the same ballets,' I said.

It wasn't a question of rights and wrongs. As people, we all have different preferences for what we do and don't like. I considered it an incredibly worthwhile experience, for if there is anywhere in the world that you would see ballet, could there be a better place than the Mariinsky? If you were in Rio, you wouldn't need to be a football fan to appreciate the Maracanã. If nothing else, it was a worthy event to stack in the memory on the list of things I'd seen and done.

Although we were all headed toward the hotel, the group splintered around this point as the older half kept walking while the younger half stopped at a bar called the Chilling Lounge. During the daytime, I usually felt more aligned with the older group, but in the nighttime, however foolish it may be, I preferred rekindling my youth and staying tight with the younger crowd. I always believed that every moment spent travelling should be maximised, and perhaps this ideal motivated my choice. As much as I felt past the nightlife scene our younger friends would seek, it felt like a more authentic way of squeezing everything from our trip than returning to our hotel. I wasn't sure how long we'd be staying out with them, but for a little while at least, it seemed the best option.

One of the highlights of any group tour is the interaction with your other travellers. People often steer clear of it, but that goes against the essence of travel. You travel to see new things and to broaden your horizons. Nothing broadens the horizons and exposes you to something new more than different people from different places. Yes, the city you were in gave you a host of them, but the people you travelled with gave you a whole other subset. We'd already spent a lot of time with the same few people on this trip, but we chatted with Cherie at the Chilling Lounge. She was another Australian, so you might think that wasn't anything new, but nationality is only so much of a link. She was from a country town four hours out of Brisbane. She came from as far away from us as Saint Petersburg is from Paris. As a young country Queenslander, her Australia had little in common with the Australia of a middle-aged urban couple from the South like us.

Cherie was midway through a similar European trip to ours, but her itinerary seemed to be in the opposite direction. She was also leaving for Helsinki after this trip, but then she was going to Germany, where we had previously been, while we were then on to Italy, where she had just been. We may find different highlights in each place, yet the ultimate of any type of experience tends to cut through to everybody.

'I always hated formal education,' Cherie said, 'but travel makes me want to learn more than anything else. Everything. I mean history, for example. We spent so long learning about World War II at school that everything seemed meaningless. You walk through the actual battle-grounds here, and it's like, right in your face. It blows you away.'

'Watch the news at home, and the little thing down the road gets more attention than war breaking out on the other side of the world,' I say. 'People take in what they can relate to. Travel gives you the ability to relate to so much more.'

'To be honest, I regret not making more of my education now that I'm getting to understand and appreciate what it was about more,' she said.

CHAPTER 18

May 1945

EKATERINA

'Why would you go to school? The most important life lesson is survival; experience is the best teacher. In ten years of life, you have had the worst battle in human history occur right outside your door. You have lost virtually every member of your family. Only we survived. Nobody can teach us about survival. We are survivors, and we need to keep surviving. Schools are good for some people, but we must react to what life has dealt us. We must do what we have to every day to keep surviving. Our lessons have been taught. The words and deeds of our families are the lessons we heed.' Dasha was determined to keep me at home.

'When others fled the city, they stayed. That two of us survived shows they were right. Targeted strikes killed many who fled. Others perished through starvation, disease and hypothermia on the road to a freedom they never reached. Even then, some who survived aimed to return once the city was liberated, only to be killed by land mines.

'That is your history class, Ekaterina. And for maths, I tell you that we would have died from starvation if we'd not been able to claim the additional rations of family members after they had died. Three hundred grams of bread a day will not allow survival, but two lots of three hundred grams is six hundred grams, which can make all the difference. What other lessons do you want?'

'I want to be able to read and to write,' I told her. Through the horrors of my childhood, the one thing I developed was the ability to tell stories. I knew the best way to do this in the future was to be writing. Babushka had taught me a little, but like Dasha, I was already behind where I should be at this age, and I didn't know how far I'd get without schooling.

'You always read. You don't need to learn much more that way,' she said. 'In time, we may be able to turn to our dreams, but for now, we must focus on realities. We need to get by any way we can. Nobody will ever want to know your stories because they are the same horrific stories everyone else has lived through.'

Throughout the war, survival was challenging, yet we could make things work by following the standard processes of the day. Whoever you were, you had a ration card that dictated what you received. You turned up, supplied your card and received what you were entitled to. As the city returned to normal, how would this work? How could we, as children, survive on our own? Without money or any way of accessing it, how do people get what they need to live? We had endured many survival lessons throughout our childhood, but they were specific to the nature of the times we had lived through.

An army unit arrived at our house one day. They demanded to speak to our guardians.

'Nobody else is home at the moment,' Dasha said.

'Who lives here?'

'My mother, my aunt and my babushka,' she said.

'Yulia Belyakova? Olga Komarova?' the soldier asked.

We had believed that we'd be left to our own devices. We expected nobody to step in our way, but the army's arrival and their knowledge of our relatives and the fate they had met suggested otherwise.

'Yes,' Dasha said.

'They are not coming back, are they?' With everything that had happened in the city, it had been impossible to account for everyone correctly. Bodies had been thrown into mass graves, and there was no thorough analysis of who these people had been. As children, we assumed this meant no accounting for anyone, but this was not true.

'Yulia Belyakova died in the hospital. Olga Komarova was found dead on Nevsky Prospect.' It was clear from our lack of reaction that this was not news to us. Had we not been aware, there had been no thought on their part to protect us from the truth. Such was the reality for all people in this city. We had all been faced with the same sort of tragedy. We all were used to accepting the loss of loved ones as mere standard day-to-day life.

'You cannot stay here unsupervised,' a woman accompanying the army unit said. There were hundreds of homes opened during the Siege, and since that time, they have been catering to the tens of thousands of children who had been orphaned in this period. The city didn't have the facilities to look after all these children but had to be seen as providing a suitable service. We didn't want to be the recipients of such so-called state generosity, but it was an obligation, not an offer.

'Unless a suitable alternative exists, you will be cared for in a state-run orphanage,' the woman said.

'What about Babushka?' Dasha asked.

'Where is she?'

'Collecting rations.'

'We shall wait,' the woman offered, but we knew there was no point continuing with that approach. Dasha turned to me, knowing that we had no options, but she was unwilling to relent and accept any requirement for supervision from anyone else.

'We have stayed here for months on our own. We need no assistance.'

'It is not for you to choose. Our records show you are fourteen, twelve and eleven. We do not make the rules, but we enforce them. You will come with us. Which girl is not here? Our records say Anastasia, Dasha and Ekaterina live here.'

'We'll have to wait for Anastasia. I'm not sure when she will be home. Anyway, we will not go with strangers. We have learnt better than that.'

As much as Dasha was determined to find a way out of the situation these people were enforcing on us, I knew there was little point in protesting inevitable decisions.

'Where will we go?' I asked.

'You will be well looked after. You will be housed in an institution where you will be well fed, educated, housed together and given the best of everything moving forward in your life.'

They told us we could have a few hours to accumulate anything we wanted to keep, and they would be back to collect us in the afternoon. When we looked outside a little later, it was evident that they weren't trusting us not to try and make an escape, for a soldier remained in the street outside our house.

'We will be looked after better than we can look after ourselves,' I said.

'Don't be fooled, Ekaterina. They won't look after us at all. It will be the job of some people to tick a box that says they look after us, but they'll do what they feel like. If they want to hurt us, they'll do it. We may have struggled alone, but at least our fate was in our own hands. Now, we are dependent on the actions of others, just as we have been through the purges that took our fathers to the war that has taken the rest of our family.'

Dasha and I had lived almost identical lives. Separated by a little over a year, we had lived in the same house surrounded by the same family unit. We'd lost the same people simultaneously, and as our family unit shrunk most significantly, we became more essential to each other. Through it all, it didn't make sense to me how different the experiences had made us. We'd both been torn apart, yet I clung to every possible positive. I saw this intervention as an opportunity for a new start, yet Dasha could see it only as another ending.

'Whatever happened to Anastasia, she was at least smart enough to avoid this fate.'

'She is probably already in an orphanage. When your mum died, she could have said she had nobody else, and they'd have taken her then. Maybe we will be reunited.'

'No. They wouldn't have had her on their list as living here if she was already recorded in an orphanage.'

'So you think...'

'I don't think anything,' she said, not wanting to think any more about what may have happened. Not knowing is often the worst thing in life. When people have someone go missing, they are usually desperate to understand what has happened. We've learned so much that has been so tragic. Not knowing is better. It leaves hope. It was one that may not be focussed on, but at this stage, it was as good as things ever seemed to be. The fact that the authorities knew how our mothers had died shows that many of the dead have been accounted for. The fact they believed Anastasia still lived with us does not mean for sure that she hasn't died, but it certainly seemed to increase the prospect.

'So,' Dasha said, 'if we must go, how do we put together our lives and those of our family into a small bag to carry forward forever more?'

'Isn't it the memories that we need to carry? Does anything else really matter?'

'Whether it matters is only part of the story. Whether they let us keep anything else is a bigger question.'

'We may have learnt a lot from our experiences, but there is plenty more that we will start learning. We're walking into a new world, and it will have a whole new set of lessons for us,' I said.

There were thought to be many tens of thousands of orphans in the city. If not for a hundred thousand children who had died in the past few years and a similar number who escaped the city without returning, who knows how dire the scenario would be? The city may not have been able to provide much for us as it stood, but it was something. It may not have been an opening to a better tomorrow, but it offered at least the potential for something more in the future.

CHAPTER 19

January 2, 2022

ADAM

My head was in my hands most of the time. I'd had tears in my eyes on a few occasions, and looking across at Louise, I could see she had, too. At least, it seemed that there was a turning point for her. She may have lost almost everyone, but as she was going on eleven years of age, it was early enough to have a genuine new start in life.

Ekaterina excused herself to go to the bathroom, and I asked Yuri a bit about their modern political landscape.

'Power operates somewhat differently here than in the West,' he said.

'You have elections, though.'

'Yes, but they are somewhat for show. When one man has enough power, he controls the wealth, the media, the military and the justice system. With that, the government never becomes unpopular.'

'How?'

'We could invade another country and start World War III tomorrow. Rest assured, every Russian would hear an alternate version of events whereby an attack had been launched on us. In your country, elections see people oust unpopular governments. Here, our governments control enough to ensure they remain popular. On the odd occasion when a genuine revolt enforces change, the truth of the previous government comes out following the change. History then takes a different view.'

Change at home can be subtle. Here, change was rare, but when it came, it was substantial. How could the masses make it happen? A coup? Every coup in history has required people with power to lead it, such as military chiefs. Every military chief here is looked after so well that they would never benefit from any change. Like or hate him, the president understands how people and systems work. Accumulate wealth and ensure that you use it to protect yourself by putting people who will never be a threat in the correct positions.

'When the Revolution came, the Soviet era saw the end of a monarch with absolute power, replaced by a government that thrust a representative of the general public into a similar position. We have had leaders who wielded power similar to the tsars through Lenin, Stalin, and their successors. With the dissolution of the Soviet Union, we believed we were moving towards a freer future, but we've had someone pulling the strings for so long that we've moved closer to the tsardom. Imagine the wealth to build a Black Sea palace grander than the imperial estates of this city. To completely control anyone in any way he needs. You see that through the Tsars, and it is very similar today. It's as likely that the average person in the street knows no more of what the government does today than they did centuries ago. As a Westerner, I suspect you cannot grasp how that could be possible.'

'How do you ever get a change?' I asked.

'You don't. You make the best of what you have. We may be better off with a different system, but fighting it is futile. Listen to Ekaterina's story. Her family needed the Siege to end to make life better. But those who actively fought it died. Those that made the best, hiding in the basement, survived.'

'They all did what they had to, right?'

'Da,' Yuri said. 'If nobody fought, the tanks would have rolled through, and everyone would have died. I am not saying there is never a time to fight for something better, but you must understand the right time for the right action. Our political situation is such that for people of my generation, getting involved is not the right approach.'

With Ekaterina still not back, I got everyone another drink and a few more pyshki to share and left Louise talking about the school system in the city with Yuri.

I reflected on the turbulent times the world has faced since 2020. In and out of lockdown, with all the border closures and restrictions that had impacted us during the pandemic, it had been different from what our generation and younger had ever known. We got upset when we had to wear masks and couldn't go wherever we wanted. Eighty years earlier, there was a city where people had 872 days of far greater restrictions. These weren't the result of government advice regarding a virus that may have got them sick, but the constant surrounding of death through bombings, starvation, hypothermia and disease. That was only a small part of the impact which had seen cannibalism, rape, murder, and pillage take over. I feel embarrassed about my complaints of being locked in my heated home with delivered groceries, entertainment and the ability to go outside safely for well-being purposes.

I knew these restrictions had been less significant in Russia than we'd faced in Australia. Still, another set of freedoms here was permanently more restricted than we took for granted.

When I got back to the table, Ekaterina was returning. 'Yuri,' I asked. 'Can you please ask Ekaterina what the impact of the past couple of years has been on her?'

'Through the pandemic, you mean?' he asked.

I nodded my head, and he began to translate my query. She looked dismissive, waving her hand at his words.

'I shouldn't have lived to eight, yet here I am on the verge of eighty-eight. What was I going to be worried about? I will live as long as possible, but if I am not genuinely living, then I just exist. What, then, is the point? I did that as a child to make it to my future. I am too old now for a future. I must live now for the present. The threat of the pandemic paled into insignificance alongside the traumas of my childhood. If it is meant to take me, it will, but I was never going to let it stop me from living how I choose for whatever time I have remaining.'

Life is a combination of what happens to you and how you deal with it. The ability to handle crises best comes from being exposed to them. The rates of depression for millennials in Syria, having grown up through the atrocities of the civil war, are lower than those in Western countries that have never faced genuine crises. Of course, everyone gauges tragedy through their own lens; the worst events of someone's life set the paradigm for how we measure tragedy. I know that by comparison with many people, I have lived a charmed life, yet I have still known tragedy and heartbreak. With such different conditioning in these ways, it is no wonder that when we arrive at the next stage of turmoil in life, my resilience carries me nowhere near as far as it does for Ekaterina.

How do you compare tragedies? Through World War II, there was so much senseless tragedy that it is hard to say who suffered most, but the scale of the carnage caused by the Siege of Leningrad was not surpassed anywhere. The twin atomic bombs that struck Hiroshima and Nagasaki to end the war are often considered the ultimate sign of destruction. Between those two blasts, the death toll was nearly a quarter of a million people. As horrific as this sounds, it is only about a quarter of the death toll from the Siege. Comparing the suffering achieves nothing. As a society, we can look at all events like these and hope lessons are learnt. We haven't seen a follow-up from those atomic bombs or anything quite like the Siege of Leningrad ever since. Still, we continue to see genocides and strategies of warfare that are similarly horrific and can never be justified. The people calling the shots were not the ones paying the price in this city, and in the battles that have occurred ever since, the same still applies. It is much easier to fight when you are risking the blood of others.

The death toll is an overly simplistic way of measuring a tragedy. A million dead doesn't begin to say anything of what this city and its people endured, but that is true of many similar combat zones. One can't evaluate the holocaust or any of history's most appalling genocides based purely on the number of dead.

Travel is always a quest to improve our lives through exposure to what lies beyond our consciousness. Finding the best and the worst of the world is the best way of doing this, for it is in these extremes that we can learn the most. Lessons are best derived from the examples of what we most seek and what we most seek to avoid. Saint Petersburg is so beautiful that tourists are exposed to the best of life wherever they search. The city has more of the worst of life to offer but naturally keeps these reminders hidden. There may be tributes to past tragedies, but considering half a million bodies lie in unmarked graves, the tributes seem out of proportion to the tragedies they represent.

'The revolution was less than a quarter of a century before the siege,' Yuri explained, using the opportunity to do more than translate, giving us additional history. 'The population dropped by two-thirds in five years at that stage, and the city needed to be rebuilt. For the city to be destroyed again so soon after, with 80% of the population killed or displaced, housing, factories, industry, water mains, sewage lines, streets, trams and bridges all ruined. The magnitude of rebuilding this city was enormous, but it did mean that even children could find a place in the future if they played their cards right.'

'And she did?' Louise asked.

'That is a matter of perspective, but either way, it is one I will let you draw based on how she tells the story.'

Before she was ready to start again, habit took over, and Ekaterina rose to clear a table before the staff member could make her way over there. However invested she was in sharing her story with us, she could not wholly divest herself of her ongoing role of keeping the flow through the café constant. Mission complete, she returned, and it was time to return to her story.

'So, when you were eleven, you moved into the orphanage,' I asked, working through Yuri's translation. 'Please tell me the traumatic part of the story ends here.'

Ekaterina smiled at us and began talking again.

'If only.'

CHAPTER 20

October 1946

EKATERINA

The Russian Orthodox church almost disappeared in the years following the revolution. Only a few Soviets had continued practising their faith, mostly privately. Our family had retained their faith, even if they were careful not to show this publicly. Dasha and I had been indoctrinated in the church, and though it wasn't a significant component of our lives, men like Archpriest Vasily had been among the closest and most important people we knew outside of blood ties. The church actively assisted orphans, but while various parishes housed small numbers, most of us were confined to extensive state-run facilities where the church had no involvement.

Life in the orphanage was dispiriting. Dasha and I had grown up as sisters, but this was discouraged here. In this institution, you were all children of the Soviet Union, linked with no other loyalties but to the orphanage and the motherland. Dasha and I were in different dormitories and were more closely aligned with numerous other children, allocated as we were by age and arrival date at the orphanage.

Dasha was determined to escape the confines she felt in here. While I also wanted a different life from what I had at the orphanage, I saw little prospect of a way out. I was resigned to the fact that I had no alternative until I turned sixteen.

Although we had food, the conditions in the orphanage were as cramped and confined as they had been at home, when eight of us shared the basement. Five years of this would have been unbearable, but I felt wrong complaining after the preceding five years. Hope for something better suddenly came when a familiar face from the past appeared.

'Archpriest Vasily,' I yelled at a volume destined to cause me trouble in the quiet of the orphanage hallway.

'Ekaterina!' Time and experience had changed me, not just mentally but in appearance as well. Despite this, he recognised me.

Archpriest Vasily was with a group of priests at the orphanage to discuss ways the church would ease the burden on the city's orphanages by opening its facilities to take in a small number of orphans.

'How do we get to be in the group that comes with you?' I asked Archpriest Vasily.

'There is a lot to be worked out. I don't know how those decisions will be made, but if there is anything that can be done to assist, you know I shall do this for you. Who else is here?'

'Dasha,' I said. 'Anastasia went missing after Aunt Yulia died.'

'It is tragic how commonplace death and disappearance have become in this city,' he said.

Since the revolution, the Orthodox Church of Russia had seen 55,000 churches cut to just a few hundred by 1939. Throughout the 1930s, the Purges saw many priests, monks, and nuns executed. The church was considered an enemy of the state, and many people practiced their faith in secrecy. World War II saw a change in this opposition, as the church supported the government's quest to unite all Soviets behind the war effort.

Dasha had said that the likelihood was the church would only take boys, hoping that some of these would choose the priesthood. If the church was to reach the same level it had previously been, thousands of priests would need to be trained to replace the many who have died either at the hands of the government or through the consequences of war.

'The church has roles for women too. Many of these women have also been killed,' I said, not knowing too much about this. Death had not been discriminatory in this city, so it was safe to say that this sector of the community would have been as savagely hit as any other.

We received the news no more than a month after Archpriest Vasily's visit. We would both leave the orphanage and be taken in by the church. Unfortunately, the resources weren't sufficient for us to go together, with Dasha to be taken in by Nikolsky Cathedral while I would attend the Church of the Resurrection. The time we had been in the orphanage had seen us become more removed from each other, so perhaps this was less of a problem than we had initially felt. I did, however, remember my parents' words. 'Family is everything,' they consistently said. Dasha was all the family I had. It may not be a long distance between us, but it was a distance we couldn't overcome with the click of our fingers.

'We're going to be alone now,' Dasha said.

'Not really. We will have other orphans living with us and the priests looking after everything. We'll have more care and consideration than we've had throughout all these years.'

'Family, in most cases, will do anything for you. Few other people do. I hope I'm wrong, but we might be jumping out of a bad situation and into a much worse one.'

'Father Vasily wouldn't do that to us,' I said.

'The best thing about Father Vasily is his enormous faith. The worst thing about him is also his enormous faith. He trusts that everyone is like him. They're not. We may end up lucky, but we may also end up as tools used by people with no interest in our wellbeing.'

Dasha left the orphanage the day before I did. I said goodbye with a heavy heart, not knowing when I would see my cousin again, yet retaining faith that Vasily would not take long to pull some strings for us.

'Take nothing for granted, Ekaterina. When anything seems too good to be true, that is probably a sign that it isn't true. Nobody does anything for anyone else unless they see something in it for themselves.'

I knew she was wrong. For all of the horrors we've seen, there have been people who have tried their utmost to aid and assist others without seeking any form of benefit for themselves. Whether we were going to be beneficiaries of this from the church was something I couldn't be so sure of. Still, Dasha's cynicism was such that she was guaranteed never to accept anything good being possible. I knew it was.

She told me she would find a way out and make it independently if given the opportunity. I didn't doubt she'd have the capacity to do that. We worked well together, but my part of the equation was more of the book smarts. Dasha had a sense of street smarts, allowing her to make it independently.

I wondered what would become of us once we had grown up and it was time to make our own way in the world. Would I ever find Dasha again? Would there ever be anyone I could walk through life with, or would I need to learn some of Dasha's attributes, sure that the life ahead of me would be built around self-dependence? No doubt this was a thought for further down the track. The next day, I would no longer be one of the anonymous masses in a state-run orphanage. I was on my way to being a big part of a small, tight-knit community protected by the sanctity of the church.

I knew my parents would be looking down, relieved that the church they had believed in was ready to step in and protect us both, even if our last family link was being severed.

CHAPTER 21

January 4, 2022

ADAM

There were more than a few bleary eyes this morning. We all left the Chilling Lounge not too much after midnight. Louise and I had been in that awkward mix where we felt too young to head back to the hotel when the older ones did but too old to settle in for a long night with the younger group. As the group agreed to leave the Chilling Lounge, I felt completely vindicated by the decision to have joined them. Once I realised they were all moving on to another club, sanity prevailed.

'You're not coming in, just for a quick one?' Cherie asked as we got to Putyazha, where the rest of the group were going.

'The Chilling Lounge was our quick one,' Louise jumped in with. She wasn't always the best at saying no to social situations, but I knew she would be liable to fall asleep walking home. She was so tired that leaving was the only option.

We never discovered how many extra hours the rest of them were out for, but five or six amongst our group looked like they were struggling this morning.

'Good night?' I asked Cherie as she slowly walked past us on the bus, every step looking challenging.

'The night was good. Unfortunately, nights get followed by mornings, and that isn't so good.'

It was only ten minutes in the bus before we descended a short way behind the Church of the Saviour on Spilled Blood. A week ago, we were in Moscow's Red Square and first set our eyes on the remarkable St. Basil's Cathedral. Many people see this church as Saint Petersburg's equivalent, with similar onion-shaped colourful domes. To be fair, I don't think this version quite has the majesty of Moscow's much older version.

Although I'd given it little thought, I assumed the church's name was connected to Christ's death. Lila explained that the 'spilled blood' in the title was completely unrelated to the 'saviour' part of it.

'In March 1881, Emperor Alexander II was being driven by horse and carriage along a route he took every Sunday. The course was well known, but he was so well protected that this wasn't ever considered risky. Cossacks, private guards and the chief of police were among the people travelling in the convoy on this one day. A man threw a bomb at the procession, killing one of the Cossacks, but it did nothing more than shake the Emperor mildly. He exited his carriage to survey the scene and offer care and concern to those injured while expressing his gratitude that he had been unhurt. Exposed, he was then an easy target for a second terrorist, who launched a bomb at the Tsar's feet. The explosion resulted in his legs being blown off, his stomach ripped open, and his face mutilated. He was rushed back to the Winter Palace but died shortly after.

'The Romanovs immediately decided to build a great church to serve as a memorial to Alexander II, chose where his blood was spilled and named it accordingly. The canal was narrowed so that the exact spot where the carriage stopped would end up within the church's walls.'

The church's look sets it apart from most architecture in Saint Petersburg. While it looks traditionally Russian, that same look is uncommon in this city, where most buildings are Baroque and Neoclassical. The city has always been a step more European than the rest of the country, but Alexander's tribute honours him as a Russian leader and is befitting of more than the standard look of the city.

'How do they ever hold a mass in here?' I asked when we walked inside.

'No masses here,' Lila said. 'It is a church in name, but it was never consecrated as a church. It is a memorial to Alexander II. It has been used for some other memorial services, but mainly, it has served as a museum. Don't forget that the Russian Orthodox church has barely existed for much of the last century. The government couldn't tear down such iconic structures, but they needed to be used for something other than worship since such honour of anyone other than the authorities was not welcomed.'

In many European cities, places of worship are prominent on the attractions list, yet often, the general feel of the city indicates that faith is very selectively practised. Given that we had so many other churches and cathedrals on the list of places to visit, this seemed in conflict with the state's anti-church approach last century.

'Your city is named after a saint, and half of your attractions are churches, yet religion is insignificant here,' Harry commented to Lila.

'It makes sense when you think about it,' she said.

Harry and I weren't the only ones waiting to hear how and why.

'Like most European cities in previous centuries, the wealth was very much in the hands of the few. Once you have everything you could need and want, you may as well insure yourself against the idea of a God by providing the best possible honours for Him. Build the brightest and brashest churches; you know it is the same in Germany, France, Spain, and Italy. We just had more of a change to our culture in the past century than those countries did.'

Every spare inch of this church's walls and ceilings was covered with stunning mosaics. Apparently, more than 7,500 square metres of them are more than any other church in the world.

The church was ransacked after the revolution and was closed a decade later. It reopened as a morgue for the masses dying from starvation, disease and combat. Although the war damaged the church, it was not severely impacted enough that it could not be repurposed in the post-war era. Initially, it became the world's most stunning warehouse as Leningrad began rebuilding, in part through agriculture. By 1970, there had been enough progress in relations between the church and the state that the decision was made to give control of the church to Saint Isaac's Cathedral. At this point, repairs and restoration began, returning it to its original glory. Ever since, it has served as a museum.

People talk about all three downtown churches, this one and the two we were headed to from here, Kazan Cathedral and Saint Isaacs. Beyond that, there is also the Naval Cathedral, the Peter and Paul Cathedral, the Trinity Cathedral and Kronstadt. It can seem like the city is dominated by the church, yet through the past century, there have been few places where the church has been less significant.

The Russian Orthodox Church's relationship with the Soviet Union seemed to depend on the government's needs at any given time. During the revolution, the Church was an enemy to crush, while it was an ally to promote during the war. It grew to be a propaganda machine for Stalin in the post-war era, but when Khrushchev came to power, it was again the enemy of the state. Parents who were banned from attending church services were forbidden to teach religion to their children. Clergy members were frequently arrested and sentenced to prison on questionable charges, reducing the church's position through the Soviet Union.

When you visit the cities of Western Europe or the Middle East, you inevitably end up seeing many places of worship, for they are at the forefront of the culture of these cities and countries. Here, the same cultural influence is missing, yet the prominence of the places of worship is the same. Could you imagine Moscow without Saint Basil's? Despite their minimal role in life here, Saint Petersburg's landscape owes a similar debt to its cathedrals and churches.

There is little interest in churches for many atheists, but I find it fascinating to see how people are so heavily influenced by belief. This building is the most iconic landmark in the city. It was planned to be a place of worship, yet it has never performed that function. It is a monument in name to both Christ and a tsar. The tsars were eliminated thirty-five years after Alexander II's assassination, while in the eyes of the Soviets, God faced a similar fate in the ensuing years.

I'm not staunchly committed against anyone's beliefs. I know how much the various churches have done to aid and assist people throughout history, but I'm equally aware of the enormous amounts of evil that have been done, supposedly in the name of God.

Whether in Saint Petersburg or elsewhere, the so-called blessed people of faith have genuinely ruined some lives.

CHAPTER 22

February 1948

EKATERINA

Eight orphans were housed in the Church of the Resurrection on the banks of the Obvodniy. Dasha's new home was at the parish of the Nikolsky Cathedral. Although the distance between us wasn't great, we had few opportunities to be away from our home parishes.

We were split into two small rooms, with four girls sharing a room large enough to accommodate four beds and little else. From the perspective of space, we were no better off in the parish than we had been in the orphanage, but it was other factors where the advantages were apparent, principally in terms of education. We had books to read, mostly donated to the church and salvaged from any possible source. We were instructed daily in history, literature, religion, language, mathematics and science. We had limited freedoms, but this was a small price to pay, especially as our education was complemented by clothing, warmth and, most wonderfully of all, regular and reliable meals.

I had been in the parish home for over six months before first seeing the price we had to pay. Archpriest Ivanovich and Priest Konstantin used to organise educational trips outside of the parish for us. Without fail, one orphan would be left at the parish as punishment for some form of disciplinary failure. One of the priests would stay behind to ensure the orphan was suitably punished. It was strange to see this happen, for none of us ever did anything wrong, or at least not that was apparent to me. We were all grateful to be in a better living situation than we'd ever known, all young enough to have no memories from before the war. We had all been given a second chance at life, and nobody would sacrifice that by breaching behavioural standards imposed on us.

Eventually, it was my turn for punishment. In this instance, I could say with certainty that it was not the result of any indiscretion on my part. Archpriest Ivanovich stayed behind to supervise me and did not attempt to suggest what I had done wrong. Soon after the rest of the house had left, he began trying to touch me the way that boy had a few years ago, when Dasha made the threat about Dad coming with a gun. When I showed my disdain for what the archpriest was doing, he made it clear that he would get what he wanted. He said it was in my best interests that I stop trying to resist. This time, there was nobody to come to my aid.

'You're only going to get yourself hurt, Ekaterina. Do you think everything comes to you for nothing? This is how life works.'

He hit me at that point, and it was increasingly rough from then on. It was the first of several times each of the priests raped me. It appeared that the way they operated was that the newest conquest became their regular choice. The other girls were spared until they became bored with me.

Priest Konstantin saw me crying in my room one afternoon while the other girls were outside. 'Your lack of gratitude is terrible. You are nothing. Despite this, you have been lifted out of the sewer to come here for this opportunity. You don't get dropped back to the same place if we let you go; you end up somewhere far worse. You make problems here, and we will make sure you have far more serious problems elsewhere. All you need to do is let us use your body as designed. Not even that often. For that, you get a life far above and beyond what the average child in Leningrad has ever known.'

We were all too afraid to say too much to each other. We weren't sure who else had experienced the same things, but I was certain I was not the only one. Eventually, I confided in Vasilyevna, who had arrived here just days before me. She seemed the closest I had to a friend.

'Has it only been the priests?' she asked.

'Yes. Who else?'

'The boys. Once the priests are bored with you, they'll pass you on to the boys. Time will tell if that is any better.'

'Why are you still here?' I asked.

'Where can I go?'

'We will work on that. But together, we can find a way.'

'Sure, just remember. I lost my mother, my father, my grandparents, my brother, my sister, my dog, and my cat. The desperation of the time meant that others among us survived by eating parts of them, and I don't just mean the pets. That is how I have lived long enough to get this far. You think repeated rapes are the worst things I've lived through?' Her story, though tragic, was typical of the time and place.

'No, me either, but we survived this long to begin a real life, not so we could start experiencing an existence just as torturous.'

I knew I couldn't put up with this. I thought of Dasha and hoped her parish was different. Dasha wouldn't have closed her eyes and cried. She would have fought back. She would have sought revenge. She would have gotten out of there if she hadn't already been thrown out after an overzealous fightback. Part of me wished I had that same fight, though I knew where it would get me. Fighting back would only have led to more dire consequences. My failure to react had at least bought me time to create a better solution, however hard that seemed to find.

When Dasha and I were on our own, however difficult things were, I always had faith that we'd make it together. Now, I am surrounded by more people but without the same feeling of complete confidence that I have someone genuinely on my side. I felt like an opportunity to bond with Vasilyevna had created an opportunity to re-establish that unity. From that, a sense of hope may grow into something more.

'How much have you spoken to the others?' I asked Vasilyevna, referring to past and present roommates. Nadia was sixteen, the oldest orphan at the church, while Kira had been here just a few weeks, taking the place of Oksana, who had left suddenly a month ago.

'Oksana told me once that the more you fight, the more you get punished. The way of survival was to accept and say nothing. That is the only escape. Nadia learnt from that example and will not say a word.'

'Are all of the boys part of this?'

'Not exactly,' she said. 'The priests' focus is on their interests. They'll use them if they believe the boys can help their best interests. If the boys are threats, then they'll punish them accordingly. Maybe the boys are smart enough to know where their interests lie, though I suspect that wasn't the case for Ilya.'

Ilya had left the church six months earlier. We were all taken to Pushkin for the day, but Ilya and Priest Ivanovich did not join us. We never saw Ilya again. We were told he had chosen to leave the church, but we never felt sure he had a choice. I suspected he may have known too much about what was happening. He would have been a threat if he implied that he would speak to a higher authority. In that case, I believed they'd have done anything to stop him from leaving unless they had very close control over where he went.

'The priests couldn't have killed him or had him killed, could they?'

'You've seen the worst of them,' she said. 'Do you doubt with all else they've done to you that they could take that extra step and kill?'

I had no reason to doubt what they were capable of. Leningrad had exposed the worst of humanity. People had no limits to what they would do to survive. In the case of these priests, their evil acts were for no reason other than inexcusable gratification. If that was the length they were willing to go to for their own benefit, how far would they go to save themselves from a life-or-death situation? Surely, they would kill.

Nadia's silence, Oksana's advice and Ilya's disappearance all seemed connected. Endure anything, say nothing and pray for the future to provide an escape. The church may have appeared to be my salvation when I came here, but it provided a broader and clearer view of life. Trust and reliance are always best retained only within yourself.

CHAPTER 23

January 4, 2022

ADAM

We didn't return to the bus before our next stop, Kazan Cathedral, which was no more than five hundred metres away. Like the Church on Spilled Blood, this cathedral had undergone its share of reinventions based on the authorities' mood toward it, but now it serves as the city's main cathedral.

Sitting on the corner of Nevsky Prospect and the Griboyedov Embankment, the onion-shaped domes of the church we'd just visited were still visible upon our arrival. The Kazan Cathedral couldn't look more different; this is closer to the Catholic cathedral in the Vatican. It was controversial when designed in the early 1800s, as there were always great distinctions between Catholic and Orthodox churches. Two centuries later, it served as a fantastic sight on the city's main street for someone focussed on aesthetics rather than religious symbolism.

As a functioning church, we were only given a brief look inside. When we returned outside, Lila told us more about the history.

'At one stage, this was the museum of atheism,' she said. 'The authorities closed the cathedral in the 1930s and decided the appropriate use was a building designed to show everything associated with religion and do it in such a light as to present the absence of faith as salvation. Of course, their push against religion was only based on pushing towards something else: the Marxist regime that ruled the Soviet Union.

'The cathedral was named in honour of Our Lady of Kazan, an icon in the Orthodox Church who represents the Virgin Mary and is considered the protector of Russia. A copy of the icon sits in the cathedral.

'The cathedral was finished in 1811, and when Russia defeated Napoleon, it became a memorial to this victory as much as it was to the icon. The commander-in-chief, General Kutuzov, was interred in the cathedral. Later, a statue of him was added in the square out front. Other symbols from this battle appear throughout the cathedral.'

The combination of war memorial and cathedral seemed counter-intuitive. Did they say masses with Christian demands like '*thou shalt not kill*,' before celebrating their people killing so many? Situations can require philosophies to be altered, but usually more discreetly than this.

Our bus awaited us outside the cathedral for the short trip to Saint Isaac's Cathedral. Saint Isaacs promised us the most comprehensive view of the city. Although we were still a few minutes away, the famed gold dome had come in and out of our view on multiple occasions. Given all the religious buildings we'd seen of late, I was less interested in the cathedral itself but couldn't wait to climb the steps and admire the view from the 360-degree walk outside on the colonnade.

The bus let us out across Saint Isaacs Square from the cathedral, adjacent to another horse sculpture. This one was a tribute to Nicholas I. The monument is right in the middle of the square, surrounded by buildings, the most famous of which is the Mariinsky Palace. The Mariinsky Palace is used today to house the local government of Saint Petersburg. It became particularly prominent when the coup of 1991 began the dissolution of the Soviet Union and the movement forward to democracy.

Of course, the most prominent feature here is the cathedral, its gold dome, one of the most famous sites in the city. Typically, for a religious building here, its history is not entirely dominated by the functions of the church. It was completed in the mid-nineteenth century, but in the early 1930s, it stopped being used as a place of worship. At the same time as the Kazan Cathedral became a museum, so did St. Isaacs.

I was drawn to the people walking along the colonnade as we crossed the square. Because the city is built without skyscrapers, the view from up there will be far more all-encompassing than most similar spots worldwide. While there may be substantially higher viewing platforms, the extra height isn't entirely beneficial. The higher you get, the less detail you can see, so the main advantage of the height is ensuring you are above all other nearby areas. In Saint Petersburg, this colonnade should be sufficient to achieve this.

Although striking from a distance, the cathedral became increasingly more impressive as we got close, despite losing sight of its crowning dome. The detail in the decoration of the facades, the massive granite columns and the incredibly detailed statues surrounding the building were all typically ornate. We did a lap of the building before entering, getting an idea of its scale. The two sides and the back of the cathedral all replicate the front, with red granite columns in the centre underneath bronze reliefs depicting various moments of biblical history.

'These are all different,' Lila explained. 'That previous one was the Resurrection of Christ. This one is the meeting of Isaac of Dalmatia with the Emperor Valens.'

'I've heard of Christ, but not Isaac of Dalmatia or Emperor Valens,' one of the other tourists said, similarly to what I'd been thinking.

'Not Richie Valens,' I said, unable to avoid the opportunity to be a smart-arse.

'A Roman emperor, but the more significant aspect is that this is Saint Isaacs Cathedral. Naturally, much of the decorative elements relate to Saint Isaac. The story depicted here is that Emperor Valens was a heretic plotting a military campaign against the Goths. Isaac had a prophecy that Valens would die in flames because of this action. The emperor was outraged and had him thrown in prison, vowing to put him to death when he returned from the battle. Valens, however, was killed, dying in a fire when taking refuge in a barn.'

'He wasn't Russian, was he? What's the connection between Isaac and Russia?' I asked.

'No. He was called Isaac of Dalmatia based on the monastery he founded in Constantinople, or Istanbul as it is now known. However, it was said that he was probably from Syria originally. The connection here is about dates. Saint Isaac's feast day is May 30, which was Peter the Great's birthday, so he adopted Isaac as the patron saint of the Romanov dynasty. It was the obvious name when it came to establishing a grand cathedral in Peter's City.

The cathedral was designed to accommodate 14,000 people. When Lila told us that outside, I didn't believe it. Once I walked in, I appreciated its enormity. We only spent a little time admiring the internal wonders, the typical mosaics that were part of all Orthodox churches, paintings, sculptures, and decorative stones. More unusual for an Orthodox church was the stained-glass window by the altar.

Although we always walked a lot while we were away, it didn't quite balance out our over-indulging. When we managed to make it to the colonnade after three hundred stairs, I felt it. Stepping outside, the feeling of fatigue was forgotten quickly. Initially, the feeling of absolute bitterness from the cold took over, but this too was quickly replaced by awe, as the view of the city from forty-five metres up was spectacular.

We took our time, slowly making our way around the entire circumference of the colonnade. Having the opportunity to view the city from every angle was amazing. The only impediment was the inclement weather, but even in this regard, we weren't hampered badly. The snow had stopped, but the cloud cover was so low that visibility didn't stretch too far. Louise could still capture some great shots from the top, including the Hermitage and the Peter and Paul Fortress.

We made our way down, conscious that others in the group were still behind us. I'd been in such a rush to get outside for what I considered the main reason for visiting the cathedral that I'd neglected to pay too much attention to what was below. Barring a couple of funerals and weddings, I haven't been to a church at home for decades, yet I'm up to three for today and perhaps fifteen in our few weeks in Europe. No doubt there will still be more to come. It never would have been on my wish list, but stripping away the religion, it is impossible not to be impressed by the architecture and artistry of these buildings. In most cases, whatever inspired their construction, they are now more museum than church. Even visiting Saint Peters in Rome, Notre Dame in Paris and Westminster Abbey in London, we have been amongst crowds of tourists who are almost oblivious to the fact they are places of worship for others.

After a quick perusal of the majesty on the walls, we made our way to the exit, where Lila was starting to show the typical worry of a tour guide: the knowledge that some in the group will always take longer than they've been given.

Momentum is part of everything. Winning and losing. Good news and bad. Our day had been one church to another, while yesterday, it was one palace to another. These patterns appear in all sorts of ways throughout life, leading to sayings like bad things happening in threes. Of course, people look for examples to prove the saying right, but there is a basis far greater than fortune. With the worst things in life, being a victim makes you more vulnerable to being a victim again. That has undoubtedly been proven true in a city like this.

CHAPTER 24

July 1949

EKATERINA

I endured the ongoing sexual abuse at the church for over twelve months. As forecast by Vasilyevna, it transitioned from the priests to the boys after a while. She and I had an ever-strengthening bond, and it was only through the support we gave each other that I retained a belief that we could make it through.

Inevitably, I fell pregnant. It had happened several times within the parish but was naturally dealt with before the wider community became aware. Abortion was illegal, but there were always ways of achieving the necessary ends. The priests had faced this situation enough times to know all the ways and means of achieving what they deemed necessary.

When Nadia left the church, she was replaced by another younger girl, and the grooming process began immediately. At this point, Kira began to take over from me as the focus of the priests while I was being subjected to more frequent and, at times, more violent sexual demands from the boys. The new girl, Xenia, was oblivious to her surroundings like we all had been on arrival. The plans in place for her demanded that she develop trust and respect for the environment and an appreciation for the opportunities that came with it. Those of us further advanced in our time here paid the price, with the only potential salvation waiting for the point when these younger girls became their primary targets.

Vasilyevna didn't yet seem to be spared from the abuse, so it seemed only departure could protect us.

Finally, matters reached a point that demanded action. Vasilyevna was violently attacked soon after falling pregnant again. Rather than sending her to their usual people for an illegal abortion, they handled the matter in-house. Taking the rest of us out, Vasilyevna was left alone with the two oldest boys. All day, I was filled with the fear that the boys would be forcing a miscarriage through a brutal bashing, but when we returned, it was apparent that I had misread the plans. Vasilyevna was gone.

'Where is she?' I asked Igor, the oldest and most fearsome of the boys.

'Who?'

'You know.'

He refused to say anything more, so I spoke to Archpriest Ivanovich about my concerns regarding Vasileyvna.

'She decided to leave us. She is sixteen now and is free to make her own decisions. We assisted her with her situation, and she chose that as the time to leave. When you are sixteen, you may choose to do the same thing. Until then, you will remember your place.'

I doubted everything he said. Why did this happen when the priests were both out? I believe they told the boys to eliminate the problem, and that was not so much the fetus as the young woman carrying it. By eliminating her, there was no need to worry about the abortion. I'm sure if they sought to get rid of her, there would only be one place they'd have considered, and though I wasn't going to dig up the yard to prove it, I prayed for her soul.

I couldn't stay there. It seemed they were working on a perpetual plan of replenishing their stock of orphans. When they were ready for a younger, fresher target, they would do the same thing to me. It was six months until I was allowed to leave, but I couldn't wait that long. I was leaving of my own accord, and whatever it took, I was going to survive on my own.

At sixteen, I would be entitled to a level of government housing, support and assistance, or potentially to be provided with a job. At fifteen, the same options didn't exist. I was to be the responsibility of a designated individual, or else I was to fly under society's radar.

It had been the intention of Dasha and I to live that way when the war ended. Now, I was facing six months of the same conditions I'd anticipated for six years, albeit without another person to share the experience. I didn't know where to go or how to make it work, but I had to escape where I was.

There was no security within the church, so the difficulty in escape was not getting out of the facility but how I could survive once outside. I would have nowhere to go, and I knew nobody who would be able to assist me. With virtually nothing to my name, how would I survive once I had escaped the church?

On one occasion when Archpriest Ivanovich had raped me in his room, he rushed out after hearing a noise. I noticed a container with money on a sideboard. I knew that the severity of punishment for stealing would be more than I could handle, but I guessed that if the sum was small enough, it would go undetected. I'd never had money, with ration cards being the only currency we used in my younger years. I took a three-ruble note, hid it in my shoe and made my way back to my room. Nothing was ever said, and I knew from that point that further opportunities would come my way if I was careful.

As sure as I had stolen some money, it would be stolen back from me without the utmost care. I cut a hole in the lining of my winter coat and kept any money I could take inside it, sewing the hole back up each time I needed to add more. Over a month, I had accumulated ten rubles. I had no idea how far that would get me, but it would at least be a starting point to buy some small amounts of food to get me through the first few days. I couldn't afford to keep taking the risks of stealing from the priests, nor could I face enduring the horrors that they were inflicting on me. If they did this without knowing of my indiscretions, what would they do once they had found me out?

Archpriest Ivanovich was away from the church for a couple of days, and I was adamant I would be gone before he returned. The boys and Priest Konstantin wouldn't be allowing me to walk out the door, but it was one less person I needed to avoid when I made my move. Although it was as simple as walking out the door, by day, we never had a moment to ourselves where we could do this, and by night, the doors were locked and accessing the keys was virtually impossible.

We had lessons in the morning, and I spent this time doing all I could to appear unwell. I forced myself to vomit. The teacher sent the other children outside to continue class while I was told to clean up the mess and then return to my bedroom to lie down. I did as instructed, but not before packing my few possessions into a bag, fully dressed and under the covers. I couldn't leave at this point, as the only way out was past Konstantin's office. I had to wait for him to disappear to the back of the facility, hopefully not noticing my presence in the bedroom, then praying that the front door of the church was open. I also knew that our teacher would be returning to check on me. I was reliant on his timing not coinciding with Konstantin's movements.

Within an hour, it happened. I saw Konstantin walk past, counted to ten, then got out of bed and picked up my bag. I peered around the corner, made my way towards the front of the living quarters, and quietly opened the main church door. A woman was standing not far from my entry point but was too busy in prayer to notice me. I quickly made my way to the exit and, after opening the main door and seeing daylight, began to run. I had no idea where I was going, just that I had a gap of no more than a couple of minutes before they came looking for me. My only objective was to get as far away as I could.

I crossed the first bridge I came to. At each intersection, I alternated between turning left and right, making the combination of turns as difficult as possible to predict. For as long as I could, I alternated between a run and a brisk walk until I felt it was impossible to continue. By this time, I had made it to the Moskovsky Victory Park, with no idea where that was in relation to the familiar points of the city.

How hard would they search for me? Would the priests fear that I would raise the alarm about what they were doing? Would the word of a desperate orphan be considered against that of holy men? I meant nothing to them like the girls who had come before me. I was a piece of meat that they'd happily discard on their own terms when they chose, so perhaps they wouldn't waste too much time looking for me now. Of course, they wouldn't have been happy, but when someone seeks to disappear, finding them is always easiest in the immediate moments. Leningrad is a huge city. After hours had passed, finding an individual was like looking for a needle in a haystack. As I sat under a tree in the park, I hoped that the effort in finding me would exceed the reward and that life would carry on at the church without me.

I had never really known free life in the city of Leningrad. I was seven when the Siege began. Since then, life has been bound by the confines of the basement, the orphanage and the church. Brief ventures to see the outside world had only been small tastes dominated by danger rather than freedom, so it had remained largely a mystery. Most frighteningly, it was a mystery I would be forced to work through alone.

At the war's end, there was an expectation that the hero city of Leningrad would be given everything necessary to rebuild stronger and better. Stalin, however, tended to view the city that had turned the war his way into a city of suspicion. Resources were prioritised for rebuilding Moscow, Kyiv, Odesa and Stalingrad. Leningrad could wait. In the meantime, the NKVD became heavily active in the city, bringing back similar policies to what had been seen through the pre-war purges. In the same way, the church was again beginning to lose its place under Stalin's post-war Soviet society, the city of Leningrad was considered an equal threat.

Against this backdrop, the city had seen limited development. Housing was being built, but it was all a one-dimensional style of tall, dull, repetitive communal apartment buildings throughout the suburbs. Despite the massive fall in population, the available accommodation was also significantly reduced. Attempts to boost the population fast were challenged by the living conditions available. I knew living on the street would not be such a problem through summer, but I needed to find contacts and a way forward quickly before winter came and life on the street was not survivable.

I was on the street for only a short time before I met Irena. She saw my condition and felt sympathetic towards me. As I got to know her, I understood why. She had been through circumstances very similar to mine. Now that she had come out the other side, she wanted to help someone going through similar trauma. She gave me a place to live and the support I needed. As limited as it was initially, I did what I could to assist her and her housemates. Once I was on my feet again, I could contribute significantly more.

I began working outside of the city, just near Pushkin. Irena and two other girls from our apartment already worked there, and the need for more resources was significant. There were still thousands of armed land mines that the Nazis had left, and while the Armed Forces were occupied on higher level tasks, the risk of dealing with these was left to girls like us. We were essentially volunteers but were given meals and bonus vouchers for our work.

The danger of getting close to people was apparent not for the first time in my life. Disarming landmines was not the safest job, and multiple girls from our brigade paid a severe price. This varied from severe injury and disability to death, but fortunately, Irena and I avoided such consequences.

As factories began reopening, finding sufficient people to work was a challenge. Through having so many co-tenants in our apartment, we had an array of people looking out for each other, so job options came about regularly. Age and experience weren't necessary, just physical capacity. With that, I had my first job, working on a production line for a machinery company. It wasn't what I wanted to do forever, but it meant an income. I could contribute to the apartment's expenses. I could pay the two kopecks for my tram fare.

By my sixteenth birthday, I had accumulated the money to fund the ultimate gifts I dreamed of. I would not do all this in one day, but throughout January 1950, I indulged in a way I never could have dreamed. First, I was able to buy a dress. I had long been confined to ill-fitting and ugly items provided by the parish or the orphanage before that. This was mine, and I adored it.

My next gift was in memory of Babushka and the game she taught us about during the Siege, where we imagined the meal of our choice in front of us. Finally, I could afford to buy pyshki and found a shop downtown that sold them. After all the years of hunger, the symbolism combined with the taste to provide arguably the most memorable meal of my life.

A few days later came my third gift, a ticket to the ballet. I saw The Nutcracker, a ballet first performed in the Mariinsky Theatre in this city. In my new dress, I looked like a proper lady and felt like the tsarina would have in the old days. It was beautiful, and as much as it made me happy, I cried. It felt like everyone I've ever lost was watching me tonight, and I didn't know whether it was wrong that I should be able to live and enjoy moments like this after the tragedies that had befallen each of them.

I felt sure it wasn't wrong, but it was part of a responsibility I would now always carry. I have survived and owe it to those who haven't to make the most of life. Retaining the memories and marking them with respect is essential, but that doesn't have to conflict with experiencing life in any way I can.

My final gift was the best of all. Once again, my new dress was on as I ventured on my day off to Palace Square and paid my entry fee for a ticket into the world's greatest museum.

The Hermitage.

CHAPTER 25

January 4, 2022

ADAM

When we first booked the Russian component of our trip, I immediately looked at a map of Saint Petersburg and worked out where we'd go on our arrival. Although we'd have days to experience all the city had to offer, there were always particular spots at the top of my bucket list that I wouldn't say I liked waiting to see. When I first visited Paris, I did a three-hour walk on arrival to see the Louvre Pyramid and the Arc de Triomphe on my way to seeing the Eiffel Tower up close. Saint Petersburg was consistently referred to as one of the world's most beautiful cities, but I realised once we'd booked that it was mainly due to the sum of all its parts; there weren't the same volume of iconic spots that defined so many other destinations.

Of course, there was the Hermitage, but as beautiful as the building may be, the true wonders were inside. Perhaps because of this, it had not warranted a late-night visit on arrival. It had ended up being relegated behind the excitement of the pyshki or at least the particular spot where we'd got them.

From Saint Isaacs, it was not quite far enough to justify getting back on the bus, yet a little further to walk than some might have liked, but the weather was clear enough now that nobody had reason to complain.

We walked through the Alexander Garden, which brought us to Senate Square and the most famous monument in the city, the Bronze

Horseman. Catherine the Great had commissioned this tribute to Peter the Great to help link herself to the city's founder. Catherine had been born a German princess, and when she took the Russian throne from her husband, who had died in uncertain circumstances, there was great suspicion surrounding her. Like a modern politician, she sought to win the favour of the people in the simplest ways. Given that she, like Peter, saw history bestow the name 'great' upon her, she achieved this goal.

The Bronze Horseman sits on a pedestal known as the Thunder Stone. It is the largest stone ever moved by humans, weighing 1,250 tonnes. The whole project was far from the quick attempt at popularity it had started, as it took fourteen years before the statue was unveiled. It came to be a landmark of the city, though. Legend stated that Saint Petersburg could never be conquered while the statue stood. Throughout the Siege of Leningrad, the Nazis brought limitless death and destruction to the city but never conquered it. The legend proved true.

We backtracked slightly into the gardens, making our way past various monuments that were pointed out and explained. When we reached the centre, we had the Admiralty fountain on our right, but our focus was to the left, on the golden spire that rose from the top of a classical Russian-style building. At the top of the spire was a ship weathervane.

'This is Admiralty,' Lila said. 'It is the headquarters of the Russian Navy and has been used for similar governmental maritime functions for the best part of two hundred years. The decorative elements of the building have all been designed to reflect that maritime aspect. Under the spire, you can see statues, right?'

We nodded as she explained that the twenty-eight statues included reflections of the four seasons, the prevailing winds and the four elements, and Isis, the protectress of shipbuilders. Spending a bit longer here would have been good, but Lila had us moving again quickly.

Palace Square was just a block away. It was breathtaking as we stepped into the massive open space with just the large central column in the middle and the two significant buildings opposite each other, their different colours offsetting each other perfectly.

'We must not stop. We will spend some time out here when we fin-ish, but we are very late for our booking,' Lila said. It had been easy to lose track of time, and a few minutes at each stop adds up significantly when you are on a tight schedule. Possibly, this tour tried to include too much while still allowing so much free time. I liked that mix, but maybe doing all three iconic places of worship and the Bronze Horseman be-fore the Hermitage was excessive.

The State Hermitage Museum is the world's largest and arguably best art museum. With over three million items in its collection, there is no way that any visit can do more than scrape the surface of all that is on offer. As part of a tour group, we're somewhat resigned to having our tastes ignored in favour of what will be most pleasing to the masses. Lila did say that we'd have a little time to wander on our own after the group tour. Given the enormity of the place, I can't see us getting far. Our main quest will be to avoid getting lost.

The birth of the Hermitage came with Catherine the Great's pur-chase of a collection of paintings in 1764. The Museum, as it was at this stage, was a private gallery in an extension of the Winter Palace. Nearly a century later, the museum became open to the public. At that stage, the collection was housed in adjacent buildings, and while the modern Her-mitage incorporates five additional buildings, the museum's main wing is the former Winter Palace.

We were quickly shown where the Egyptian antiquities section was and told that it led to the Classical Antiquities, which took up most of the ground floor and much of the Old and New Hermitage buildings. We didn't stop there, but the expectation was that this would be the sec-tion most of the group would seek out at the end of our tour, as it would be near the exit that would lead to our final meeting point.

Lila then led us up the Jordan staircase. Near the museum's entrance, this feature supposedly greeted visitors to significant state events held by the Imperial leaders when this was the tsar's residence. I didn't doubt it; the grandeur of the surroundings could surpass most of the items dis-played as we ventured further on.

When we entered the main halls upstairs, we were in an area dominated by Renaissance and Baroque Art. From the time Lila devoted to it, this was her opinion of the museum's highlight. She seemed particularly enamoured with the Dutch masters, and we spent more time looking at the works of Rubens and Rembrandt than on the rest of art history combined. Her knowledge was excellent. Rather than a tour devoted to showing us what was on display, she extensively detailed all the works we saw. She focussed far less on the museum itself and concentrated predominantly on the art history.

Given our dinner at Wine Gogh the other night, I would have expected we'd see the Hermitage's display of Vincent Van Gogh's works. The museum has nine of his paintings in its collection, including White House at Night and Portrait of Madame Trabec. While they may be far from his most famous works, any museum with paintings from the world's most renowned artist usually considers that a highlight. Unfortunately, we didn't see any of these. Likewise, we skipped Picasso and anyone else from the 20th century.

'Alright, that completes our tour of the Hermitage,' Lila said. 'We are meeting by the Alexander Column in the middle of the square at 6 pm. This leaves you half an hour to do a quick bit of exploration if there is anything in particular you want to see in the museum or to use the restrooms if you need.'

'Half an hour,' I said quietly to Louise. 'The world's biggest museum and we have half an hour. Not even that long if we allow time to get out of the door and across to the centre of the square.'

'Even less. It's already 5.33.'

I quickly checked the layout of the museum on my phone.

'Van Gogh's display is in room 413. We'd be lucky to get there by 6 a.m. tomorrow. That is way across the square in the General Staff Building.'

'I thought that had nothing to do with the Hermitage,' Louise said.

'Originally, it didn't, but you can't fit half of human history into one building. Maybe we wander back to the Egyptian artifacts and slowly meander to the meeting point.'

'Maybe that's why her tour was that way,' Louise said. 'So much territory, so she gave us an introductory look based on what was close.'

For all of the impact that the travel industry has faced in the past couple of years, you wouldn't know it in the Hermitage. There still seemed to be people everywhere. I'd never been at my most comfortable in big crowds, but when you want to experience the world's most exciting destinations, you learn to get used to them. Part of connecting with different places was connecting with different people. Avoiding getting involved with people to some extent was impossible, so the lesson was to learn to appreciate them.

CHAPTER 26

September 1956

EKATERINA

Throughout my time of independence, I had sought to avoid being involved with people whenever it was avoidable. My first fifteen years had given me little reason to believe that others who suddenly came into my life offered anything good, so I kept to myself where possible.

Irena had been an incredible asset in taking me into her home and finding me a job. She had been the one true friend I'd made since escaping the parish, but that relationship had changed over the ensuing years. She had met a man named Leonid, and in 1953, they married. From that point, she had largely disappeared from my life, the new dynamics of married life heavily changing her lifestyle. Our interactions had been diminishing with time, so it wasn't a significant issue for me when we drifted further apart after her marriage. The extra degree of freedom from interpersonal obligations was a positive. I will forever appreciate the help she gave me when I most desperately needed it, but like most relationships, there comes a point where the best times have passed, and we were there.

The first significant threat to that loving solitude came a couple of years later through a man at work named Borislav. He lived in the same apartment block as me. He caught the same train, heading from Avtovo to Narvskaya station at the same time as me each morning and returning each night. When he began talking to me at the station, I initially ignored him, but after he continued this with ongoing attempts at work and around the building, I relented.

'I am sorry, I am not the kind of woman you are looking for,' I told him when his enthusiasm grew too much.

'What sort of woman am I looking for?' he asked.

'A wife. The war changed the direction of a lot of people. I may be a survivor, but I'm not headed towards the same life that I had been.'

'Few of us are,' he said. I don't think he meant this and remained convinced of his hopes and intentions, but at least I could see he was a patient man. My experiences in the church convinced me I would never want to be with a man in such a way, but I always retained a curiosity about how such things were meant to be. Besides, if I was the only person left to carry on the family lineage that put me on this earth, shouldn't I seek to ensure that line continues?

Leningrad had become a city of women, and it was only slowly beginning to correct itself. While civilian casualties in the war included all demographics, the impact of the military losses had seen the population in the city at the end of the war stand at over 70% female. Work was available for women, so many of the peasants from surrounding areas moved into the city, and these were disproportionately female.

While some of the growing population were people returning to the city they had previously escaped, most were new. It wasn't just what we'd been through, but this new wave of people ensuring that the modern city of Leningrad bore continually less resemblance to the city of the past. I'd been too young to know it, yet I still felt a connection to the famed, beautiful city. Through all I learned from my mama and babushka, Saint Petersburg represented the forefront of progressive thinking. Artists highlight the progression of a society far more than the political class. Saint Petersburg was at the forefront of the world's greatest artists, and the political classes of the Soviet Union preferred to stifle this rather than celebrate it. Leningrad wasn't just a renamed Saint Petersburg; it was a reimagined one.

My conversations with Borislav continued to become more prolonged and frequent. I began enjoying talking to him rather than enduring it. I started talking about what I would like to do instead of what I did, which filled my heart. Like the sixteen-year-old dreamer, I was going back to the Hermitage, the ballet and the pyshki shops, but now I was letting him come with me and let him into my soul. He was taking his place in my heart as I did his. Slowly but surely, my attitude changed.

While we'd discussed so much connected to the war, most of it was generalised. He had left Leningrad at the start of the Siege and returned more than four years later. He knew that I had stayed throughout, and he was naturally aware of all that I lost through that time. He was unaware of all I suffered after the Siege, and I knew that the events and their impacts could shape everything else in the future.

'Borislav, I need you to know what happened to me. After the Siege, I was placed into the care of the church. I was raped by priests and by other orphans in the home. I was impregnated and made to have abortions, in some cases through the use of coat hangers, drugs and intense physical trauma. Whether I am physically or mentally able to be a proper wife to you is something I cannot promise. Whether I can carry a child full-term is something else I am uncertain of. I can walk away from you now and accept it as yet another loss in my life. I will overcome that now, but if you decide to remain with me, knowing all this, things will change. Once you commit, I will genuinely need you to stay by my side through life.

'You don't think that I would walk away from you due to the crimes of others?'

'I have learnt to assume little. I believe we all have to pursue what we most want in life. Whether that is best served with or without me is something only you can answer.'

He was able to answer without hesitation or doubt. He proposed soon after this, and at the age of 23, for the first time in my life, I felt like I had found myself somewhere safe. I hadn't believed belonging to someone else was a suitable aspiration, yet it felt like a valid reward for all I'd been through. It wasn't quite the most incredible love story of all time, but I had someone to walk through life with.

We were married during the White Nights of 1957. It was a wedding befitting the simplicity of the times and the small circle of people that were part of our lives. Borislav's family was small but tight-knit, while I had nobody. Irena and her husband were the only guests I had invited, and Borislav added a few of our colleagues. This small event was all we wanted. After the journey of life to this point, the concept of now being married had seemed inconceivable not so long before, so there never had been a dream wedding fermenting in my mind.

Wedded bliss. I've heard the term, but I don't know how to compare what we had with that. The emptiness within life stemmed from the evil of people and how that had permeated from them to the inner sanctum of my life. My marital status fixed none of the evils. However, there was now a space in my life that appeared free from these horrors. For now, at least.

CHAPTER 27

January 4, 2022

ADAM

'Can I ask a really stupid question, Lila?'

'Another one, Adam. Sure.'

She laughed, though I was pretty sure that nothing I had asked so far had been that unintelligent. Cynical, yes. Sarcastic, yes. Maybe the same applies to Lila's response.

'If it never gets dark in summer, why doesn't the opposite happen in winter? Shouldn't it be dark all of the time?'

'It is strange that you have asked this when it is dark,' she said. 'In winter, we get as little as five hours between sunrise and sunset, while in summer, we get the opposite. Just like anywhere in the world, those segments are considered daylight hours and night-time hours. The truth is, those terms don't cover every minute. Between those points are twilight hours. There is still a certain amount of light when the sun goes down. Because we are so far north, the sun never sets deeply enough in the middle of the summer that we lose the twilight. The same doesn't work in reverse. Although the sun only rises a a little above the horizon, it still provides full light.'

Perhaps living in an environment where days got shorter and longer, but never quite so excessively, meant I'd never really thought about this. Even on our equinox, twelve hours of daylight weren't matched by twelve hours of darkness once the twilight was considered.

'I was expecting a sillier question after that build-up,' Lila said. 'Science isn't normally my strong point, though, so if you are happy with the answer, I will quit while I'm ahead.'

She probably thought that coming out of the Hermitage and walking into Palace Square, my mind would have been far less focussed on the sequence of the sun than the more immediate experiences. That said, a week with me and she probably understood me well enough by now to know otherwise.

Europe is filled with spectacular city squares paramount to how life functions in each city. Palace Square is a little different to most of these, with its day-to-day function predominantly as a tourist hub rather than a central point for the city's citizens. It is used for significant events, such as New Year's celebrations occasional concerts and historically, for political demonstrations, such as the Bloody Sunday massacre and parts of the October Revolution.

The square is dominated by two prominent structures, the Winter Palace that we've just walked out from and the General Staff Building opposite. Although built a century apart, they look like they belong to part of the same project. Now that the Eastern Wing of the General Staff Building is used as part of the Hermitage Museum, it is directly connected to the opposite palace.

The Winter Palace was designed by Italian architect Francesco Rastrelli. He also designed the Catherine and Peterhof Palaces, so the similarity is understandable. Another Italian designed the General Staff Building, making the influence easy to see.

The General Staff Building is bow-shaped and curls around the square's southern side. It is considered neo-classical in style but sits perfectly against the Winter Palace. It offsets the turquoise and white of the Winter Palace with a bright golden colour reminiscent of Peterhof.

In the centre of the square is the Alexander Column. As the only permanent structure inside the central five hectares of the square, it is the focal point and is a further celebration of the victory over Napoleon. At nearly fifty metres, it is the tallest structure of its kind anywhere in the world. At the top is a statue of an angel holding a cross, while the pedestal is decorated with an array of symbols of military glory. It seemed to be a rare example of a monument that didn't have a horse front and centre in depicting glory.

At this time of the year, the square had one other unmissable feature. I don't know where it fits globally, but the Christmas tree was the biggest I have ever seen, sitting halfway between the Alexander column and the triumphal arch. As an Orthodox country, Christmas is celebrated a few days from now, even though we celebrated it more than a week ago in Germany. Traditionally, Russia has not been as active in its festive season celebrations as most of the West, but this is another area where attitudes have changed. They haven't embraced it precisely as we do. There is no Father Christmas, but there is Ded Moroz, which loosely translates to Grandfather Frost. Snegurochka, his granddaughter, accompanies him. She ensures that Russian men's attention remains on the festivities more than Ded Moroz does with the children.

Palace Square's magnitude was different from most equivalent spaces I had visited. Through being more open, it felt bigger. It also gave the column an even greater prominence than it would otherwise have. In many ways, it would probably be a more fitting place for the hero city column, but that didn't seem to fit with how the Russian culture apportioned recognition. Here, it seems tributes are based on the victory's magnitude rather than the level of sacrifice. This city was critical to the Allies winning World War II, but the success 130 years earlier was not one shared among other powers. That victory was Russian alone, which appeared to warrant the most symbolic recognition.

Several horse-drawn carriages were travelling around the square. The lit-up carriages were stunning, as were the horses pulling them. They were only travelling around the square, so the value of a ride was for the feeling it generated rather than any form of transportation. That wouldn't have stopped me had we been alone and without time restrictions. With a tour group and deadlines, I had to be content with a quick look as they passed us.

We were brought together near the centre of the square for a group photo. How much others valued these may vary, but I liked getting a shot of the group you travelled with. Occasionally, you stay in touch with people you meet on your travels, but most fade into obscurity. Over a week, there will be something to remember each individual by, whether good or bad. Having a photo you can look back on from time to time can be that little memory jog that allows you to tick a mental box about an individual's unique place within your life. We did a tour several years back, where we developed an ongoing friendship with some fellow Australians. Catching up last year, a name from our tour came up, and I couldn't place the person at all. I usually am very good at this, but the lack of an image to piece with the memory had seen the person disappear from my mind. Everyone can be a lesson in some way to us, so I don't want these people to disappear from my mind. Even if the negative qualities of a person teach us a little more of what we don't like in people, the role each person plays is worth hanging on to.

When we leave on Thursday, the likelihood of seeing any of these people again is minimal. Harry, Judy and their adult children have been great company, but being from the opposite side of the world, the prospect of us being in the same city again isn't high. There are plenty of other people in this group who I've enjoyed getting to know, but one of the lessons that comes from that is how people add value to your life and your experiences when you let them. People walk past each other without acknowledgement daily, anywhere in the world. It isn't natural, but we've trained ourselves to do it, unlike every other animal that looks at each new member of their species with curiosity and interest. We don't, and the bigger the city and more common the situation, the more we shun each other. Every person we value starts as a stranger to us. When we are in a class at school with people, in a sporting team, a club, a workplace, or on an overseas tour group, we are forced to interact, and when we do, most of the time, we find positive attributes that can lead to enriching experiences. However much we choose not to believe it, people are integral to making the best of our lives.

CHAPTER 28

November 1958

EKATERINA

After we married, we moved into an apartment in the city centre. It was tiny, but it was just the two of us, which at this point in the city's history was quite an achievement and one to which we owed an enormous debt to Borislav's father.

Soon after moving in, we found the ultimate place to visit after work: Pyshechnaya. It had only opened shortly before we moved into the area. Just a few blocks from home, we would come together for pyshki and coffee several times a week to taste the good life. What became infinitely better than I could ever have imagined was that throughout that winter, it wasn't just pyshki and coffee that I got at Pyshechnaya. I was offered a job.

'There is much more demand than anticipated,' the manager Kamila told me. 'We wish to stay open longer hours, so we need additional staff. The job is yours if you want it.'

As a girl, I had dreamed I would work in some creative capacity, perhaps as a writer or painter, but the Siege and all that followed had dramatically curtailed my options. I dreamed of working at the Hermitage once I first visited. There was no need for anything glamorous; being surrounded by all the magical artifacts there seemed perfect. I never imagined a point where serving pyshki would seem like the ultimate, yet it did seem far more ideal than the factory.

'I feel a deep connection to my babushka here. Parts of the little girl that weren't destroyed glow within me when I'm here. I feel, strange as it may sound, that I belong here.'

'Then you should work here, my dear,' Borislav said.

Seeing less of each other with our workplaces so far removed wasn't a significant issue. Every day started and ended in the right way, with us waking and falling asleep in each other's arms. We made the most of our free time together, exploring various interests that took us all across our beautiful city. Borislav loved to write the stories of all he found while I had received a camera from his parents, and I took the pictures to tell stories as he did with words. Though neither of us necessarily expected to make anything of this, it fuelled a passion within us and one that complimented each other perfectly.

'Dreaming of the best possible life is something we should never stop doing,' Borislav said. 'We don't set a deadline by which we have the life we want; we do what we need each day to pursue a better tomorrow. If we achieve an infinitely better life than we knew before, it doesn't mean we stop there; we should always aspire to more.'

'What do you mean?'

'Pyshechnaya is a big step forward today, but it doesn't mean it has to be forever. You may be an internationally renowned photographer down the track. Never give up on a dream, but never over-commit to it so much that there aren't other things along the way that make life good.'

Borislav worked in a supervisory role at the factory. While it had always been a workplace that he didn't mind, it was unfulfilling enough that he always maintained a desire to move forward in time. There was sufficient nepotism everywhere in this city that higher managerial roles were never achievable for someone without higher contacts than Borislav had, so his current level was as far as he was likely to go.

Borislav's family came from old money, but they were far enough down the chain that they had not been involved in any power struggles in the city. In Leningrad, any person who had benefited from power in one decade had suffered its scourge in another decade. By steering clear of the power struggles in the 1930s, they had avoided the Purge. By not looking at filling the post-Siege power vacuum, they also avoided the impact of the Leningrad Affair. Borislav was therefore left in that middle range where he was seen as no threat to anyone but equally valuable to whoever wielded power at the time.

Peter the Great's city may have been the bastion of artistic excellence, but under Soviet rule, there was little freedom or celebration of the arts. Khrushchev had certainly relaxed some of Stalin's harder-lined approaches, but Borislav wasn't convinced that a writing career was a sensible option. He continued to write stories of the city, but they remained in his journals, hidden from the eyes of the world. As I developed my own passion for photography, I found myself capturing more of the beauty of this city, both the natural and the re-emerging architectural masterpieces that had built our reputation over the previous two centuries. My shifts at Pyshechnaya generally coincided closely enough with Borislav's working hours to explore the city and develop our art in unison.

Change, however, was on its way. After the damage done to me by the priests and the orphans when living in the church home, I didn't think there was any likelihood that I would be able to have children. Eventually, we had to confront a reality we hadn't thought about. I was pregnant. Although the available medical resources in Leningrad were far too limited to give us any level of certainty, the doctors indicated that the foetus was healthy. They believed there was no reason that I wouldn't be able to give birth safely to a fully developed and healthy child.

Whatever positives had come through the past few years, life had given me enough tragedy that I wasn't feeling too confident.

'Together, we will face whatever our destiny is,' Borislav said. I loved his words, though I still couldn't grasp them entirely. We were in everything together, but it would be my fault if anything were to go wrong. Well, maybe not my fault, but the result of my past and nothing to do with Borislav. Of course, I knew his support was endless, but it felt as though that left a responsibility on me to ensure nothing terrible happened. This was one case where I had no such control.

I had to do everything possible to remove any risks, so I gave up my job at Pyshechnaya. I envisaged returning after the birth, but no protections were in place to guarantee the option. Naturally, I didn't stay away entirely, for once I no longer worked there, I craved pyshki more than ever.

For all of the fears, the labour was relatively straightforward. Yevgeny was born on March 4, 1961, without significant issues for him or me. When I first held him, the miracle of life was complete. Everything I'd been through was worth it to experience this moment.

Borislav had promised me a new life, a better life than what I had always known. From the moment we'd met, his promises had been kept. Our marriage, home, artistic pursuits and work life had brought new happiness levels, but they all paled into insignificance alongside this moment. After seeing so much life taken away from me, finally, I had created life. I was complete.

CHAPTER 29

January 4, 2022

ADAM

'Why not? We've got to eat anyway, so why not at least do so somewhere that we have a local vouching for the quality, assisting with any possible language issues and where we've got a bunch of other people to share the experience with.'

The dinner tonight was not included in the tour, so we'd pay as we went. Sure enough, this fact meant that Johannes, Marizane, and our unfriendly compatriot Trish would not be coming, though most of the tour group would. The destination was a Georgian restaurant called Khochu Kharcho, about ten minutes from our hotel down Sadoyava Street.

Louise didn't take a lot of convincing. She seemed exhausted after a long day following a reasonably late night, so I had feared that she might have wanted to stay closer to the hotel and avoid any temptation to extend the evening. I felt just as tired but hated wasting an evening when travelling. It may only be a basic dinner, but it was somewhere that we only had one chance of discovering.

'So, what is Georgian food?' she asked.

'Bordering Russia, I'm going to say you won't notice the difference between Georgian and Russian,' I said.

'At this stage, Russian only means that we have vodka before the main course, and beef stroganoff is on the menu. Besides that, I'm still unsure how to define the cuisine.'

For us, food is wholly connected to the experience of travel. Even on short trips in the country areas back home, our views of the places we visit always rise and fall based on the calibre of the food we eat. In those places, food is judged based on the restaurant, café or hotel where you dine. Still, when you step into a different culture in faraway lands, you automatically judge the country's cuisine based on your experiences in a similarly small number of establishments. It is no coincidence that we've returned so often to France and started this European trip in its capital, Paris. The hotel breakfasts disappointed us since we had arrived in Russia, but we agreed that even other meals didn't measure up to the rest of Europe.

'What about pyshki?' Louise asked to get a reaction.

'They have a special meaning to me now, but I can't pretend they equate to the kind of treat we'd find in a Parisian boulangerie.'

About half of our group came to the dinner, and we managed to squeeze onto two tables. We sat with Harry, Judy, their children Ben and Nikki, and Canadian solo traveller Jeremy. Lila joined us while we were scouring through the menus. They could have been renamed encyclopedias, as thick and extensive as they were. While so much choice often created more problems than it solved, at least it ensured nobody could say they didn't find anything they liked the look of. Language wasn't an issue; every item on the menu had clear photos to assist everyone.

'You must order a couple of Khachapuri to share,' Lila said.

'What are they?' Harry asked while I searched through the menu.

'I guess you would say they are a type of cheesy bread. There are many varieties,' she said as she found the correct page on the menu and started taking us through them. We ordered a traditional Khachapuri, an Adjarian one, which was boat-shaped and topped with an egg and a Mingrelian variety with extra cheese on top and inside, which resembled a cheese pizza.

They were fantastic; if anything was disappointing, it was how stuffed we felt before our main meals arrived. Across the table, we had a wide variety of dishes ordered. After Louise told me that ordering pancakes for dinner wasn't appropriate, I decided to go with the second-best option I could find. Having not had seafood while in Russia, I decided it was time to try, ordering baked cod and vegetables. It was far less memorable than the Khachapuri, to be honest, but good enough to be content. The stroganoff probably looked like the pick of the dishes, but it felt too clichéd. The other dish that was well received was kharcho, which, based on the restaurant's name, was no doubt another Georgian specialty. This was a thick soup or broth filled with meat and heavy spices.

'So, pancakes now?' I asked.

Nobody was even contemplating dessert, and the main topic was plans for the rest of the evening. Jeremy was checking up on the rest of the younger people at the other table, who were all keen for more Saint Petersburg nightlife. Ben and Nadia said they would join them, while Harry and Judy said they would split the difference and head to the hotel bar. We had options, but a part of me couldn't come to terms with being part of the old half of the group. I avoided committing to anything but felt the right option was to follow Jeremy, Ben and Nikki.

The group was about to lose one of our number. Jeff, the doctor from the United States who was travelling with his mother, had locked in a date using an online app while we were having dinner.

'Seriously?' I asked, showing my naivety on how much the dating world had changed in the past generation. 'You're on the other side of the world, and you can meet someone over the phone and go and um...'

'Yep,' he said, smiling and wishing the rest of us a good night. He was sure he was in for one.

Carol, his mother, shrugged her shoulders. 'You can't travel with a single son in his twenties and then complain if he stands you up when the offer of a young local woman comes along.'

Once we'd sorted out the bill, we went down the stairs and to the exit. We were all headed in the same direction, but within the same block as the restaurant, the bigger half of the group stopped at the sight of a spiral staircase leading to a bar that looked like a reasonable starting point for them. I looked at Louise last to see what she wanted to do. The pause seemed enough, and we were joining the younger group at the bar.

'Good choice,' Cherie said. 'We don't have an early start tomorrow, so why not?'

'It's an early enough start,' Louise said, 'so we're only coming in briefly.'

'Yeah, right,' Cherie said. At her age, there was no such thing as briefly when you went into a club unless you were planning on moving on to another.

There were eight of us, but before too long, we'd all integrated with others in the bar. It was tourist orientated, given that I heard more English than Russian. There still seemed to be enough of a local influence that I could listen to some of our group trying to find the best places to move on to. While this bar seemed more than hip to a mid-40s couple, the very fact I could have active conversations meant it wasn't a loud enough party atmosphere for them.

'There is a karaoke bar just across the road. A cigar bar is a block up that way, but if you want somewhere really pumping, I will say Estrada, down Sadovaya Street nearly to Nevsky Prospect,' a local guy told Cherie. 'Within a few blocks from there, you'll find many other good clubs, but it's a bit early for those places.

Trying not to be seen yawning, I finished my beer and tried to gauge what the rest of the group would do. Cherie seemed more interested in the Russian guy than in partying elsewhere, while the rest of the group was keen to head towards Nevsky Prospect.

'Now or never,' I said to Louise, at least half-hoping that she'd choose never.

'Alright. We're only young once, and seeing we missed it then, we'll pretend now,' she said.

Cherie was staying but encouraged the rest of us to go, indicating her plans had been locked in. The old man in me wasn't comfortable leaving her with a stranger in a strange city, but it was clear that she could make these decisions for herself. Louise had spoken to her quite a bit over the past few days, and throughout her solo travelling experiences, she'd had plenty of moments like these to know what she was doing.

'You weren't worried about Jeff going off on a date with someone he hadn't even met, were you?'

I wasn't going to get into a debate with my wife. Still, I muttered a theory about online dating apps' security connection, whereas the man Cherie was with could be anyone. I quickly changed topics, walking into just as much trouble by speculating on whether the young women here would be as close to undressed as the clubbers back home, given the below-zero temperatures they'd endure getting there.

'I think you'll have to go inside to perv,' Louise said. 'Cloak rooms would be far more common here. You'd have hypothermia in moments outside here in a short skirt and crop top.'

I realised my best option from here was to stay silent for a while. Travel is a learning experience, and there is always more to learn through listening than talking.

'You sure we'll find much open on a Tuesday night?' Nikki asked.

When you travel, days of the week have a different feel. Tuesdays and Saturdays felt the same, but the difference was immense in finding open and busy nightclubs. A city this size never stops, but we had to move deeper into the central heart of the nightlife zone to see what our group was after.

Most clubs here don't charge for entry, which was the case with the first suitable-looking place. With a name only written in Cyrillic, I had no idea where we were other than being a block from Nevsky Prospect. Downstairs, the bass vibrated through me, and I felt like I'd gone back a quarter of a century. My time for listening, or at least hearing, was over.

Louise managed to get a cocktail for herself and a beer for me, and while she quickly managed to find nightclub mode, I couldn't have felt more out of my comfort zone. It typified the way the two of us operated. My adventurous mindset always made me more likely to choose to do something out of the ordinary, yet once the decision was made, it was Louise who embraced it, while I hoped it would end and we'd be home as soon as possible.

I often pay a price in these environments, as once I'm uncomfortable, I keep the glass in my hand moving towards my mouth more frequently than usual. Drinks go down fast until they can't anymore. I was on my third since we arrived here when the group decided to move on to the next club. As we climbed the stairs, I asked Louise how she'd feel about staying with the rest of the group while I went home.

'What? I've wanted to return to the hotel since we left the restaurant,' she said.

'Hey, we're gonna go back the other way,' I called out to the group. I didn't want to word it in a way that sounded like we were old folks needing to head home to bed and left in terms that may have meant we were going back to the karaoke bar that was mentioned earlier.

'Cool, no worries,' Ben said. I'm sure none of them had expected us to stay out nor cared we were going. Ben and Nikki probably held back while we were there, thinking we might report back to their parents. The sensible decision for us was right for everyone.

Louise had kept going for my sake. I had kept going for hers. Neither of us wanted to look like the old fart that couldn't keep up, but each of us was feeling our age among the people a generation younger. Once we finally acknowledged this to each other, sanity prevailed. Finally, with an incredible feeling of relief, we were going home.

CHAPTER 30

February 1962

EKATERINA

Finally, with an incredible feeling of relief, we were going home. Four days after giving birth to Yevgeny, the doctors cleared us with no signs of any problems or complications. I remained nervous but was constantly reminded of how normal that was for any mother.

From the time we got home, I continually said that we should be returning to the hospital, regularly raising my fears with Borislav. Feeding was a struggle for him, and I wasn't convinced about his breathing ability. His skin seemed bluish, which I knew was a sign of problems, but Borislav was adamant that this was far too mild for concern.

It was nearly a week before Borislav accepted my fears were valid, and we returned to the hospital on a Monday morning to have Yevgeny looked at. He hadn't gained any weight the whole time he was home, and when added to the other symptoms I'd previously mentioned, Borislav accepted that something significant might be wrong.

'Anything that significant they should have seen in the first few days though, surely,' he said.

'Should, yes. It doesn't mean it's certain, though.'

The reaction at the hospital was typical. Leningrad had the resources in its hospital system to thoroughly cope with a tiny percentage of the city's needs. Assumptions were made when genuine assessments were too time-consuming and costly to determine. New parents were liable to panic, which was the preconceived notion shown when we arrived. They looked at Yevgeny but sought explanations for why things weren't wrong rather than taking the appropriate conservative approach to determining what might be wrong.

We were sent home again after several hours and given a list of things to watch out for and to return in a week if we were uncertain about his progress. I insisted that we see another doctor in the next couple of days if there hadn't been a clear improvement.

'Of course,' he said. Although he accepted what he'd been told at the hospital, there remained enough of a sense of doubt that he would be watching with closer eyes.

There was no change. His breathing remained laboured, and he still barely ate. The impact was having additional effects on me. Afraid of having him out of sight for a moment, I wasn't sleeping. Eventually, this impact had to come to a head, and on Thursday night, I collapsed on the bed. It could just as quickly have been minutes or hours later when Borislav woke me in a panic.

'He's not breathing,' he screamed.

I rushed to him despite feeling sure it was futile. He had been a miracle from the moment of conception. Despite all I had been told, I had doubted that he would survive until birth. Ever since, I have felt sure that his time with us would be fleeting, and now reality had proven me right.

For all of the failures to test thoroughly while he was alive, they were willing and able to do an autopsy that revealed the cause of death was a heart attack caused by a rare congenital defect impacting the aorta. It would have made no difference if they had been aware of it straight after birth. There would have been nothing that they could have done. If anything, we were better off not having it diagnosed, as it meant we could have the brief positive feeling of bringing him home and having the dream family house.

Both of us were beyond consolation. The losses I had known hadn't provided genuine preparation for this. I lost everyone, but this had never come after the sudden joy of arrival. Everyone I lost had effectively always been there for me. The death of Yevgeny was the first time I had lost someone I'd celebrated the arrival of. It was shattering, but as much as I suffered, Borislav took it substantially worse. For all the philosophical attitude he had shown before the birth when we discussed the significant risks, he had taken the birth as the point at which the worries were over. I always knew that the concerns were only changing rather than ending.

Alcohol soon became Borislav's crutch. It was rare for people to be given time away from work, irrespective of how dire their situations were, but he was given a leave of absence for a few weeks. Rather than use this time for any constructive means of making progress, he spent all of his time drinking, only stopping once he was unconscious.

'What do we do?' I asked him.

'What do you mean?'

'This is reality. We can't escape it. We can't bring him back. What does this mean for the rest of your life? You can't continue like this.'

'The rest of life may not as well exist, for all I care.' His words were somewhat prophetic, as the rest of his life didn't exist much longer. Borislav was killed less than a month after Yevgeny's death. He was struck by a train. The apparent thought was that he jumped in front of it, but his alcohol consumption was so substantial that it was common for him to lose balance. I suspect he fell rather than jumped, but what difference does it make? He had lost the desire to live, and whether he had chosen the way out was merely a technicality. His approach to life had reached a point whereby destiny was final. His lack of desire to live led to his death. The semantics of the cause of death were largely irrelevant, yet for some reason, a feeling within made accidental death feel better to me. After the continual losses through life, the idea of anyone choosing to leave would be harder to comprehend.

His death was officially accepted as an accident, saving me significant headaches. When we got married, Borislav had taken out a life insurance policy. Whether they would pay out on a suicide was questionable.

Without him, I was dependent on this money. While the proceeds of this weren't enormous, it left me in a comfortable enough position that there was no need for me to work in the short term. Although impacted less by the loss of my husband than I had been when my son died, I wasn't ready to engage with the outside world, so this financial position was a great relief. I couldn't completely shut myself off from the world, though, as everything that needed to be done had to be done by me. There were no friends or family to aid and assist me in any way. I had to shop. I had to pay bills. I had to coordinate life, as simple and one-dimensional as this life may have been.

Living a couple of blocks from the city's busiest thoroughfare seems unsuitable for someone wanting to avoid people. Still, the thought of going through the ordeal associated with moving was worse. Anything that needed doing outside of the house was rushed and dealt with as quickly as possible. Thankfully, I was just a few blocks from the Metro, so I would get the train from Nevsky Prospect and make my way wherever necessary across town before rushing home as quickly as possible.

After Borislav's death, many people might expect I'd have avoided trains at all costs, but that was far from the case. The Metro seemed to be a place of refuge for me, perhaps symbolic of my life. It had become a new part of the city in the 1950s, just as I was discovering my new life. It was underground, just as I had spent those formative years during the Siege. It felt hidden there, just as I had needed to be when escaping the Church. Although it was where Borislav died, it was also where we met, and that carried a more powerful memory to me.

I often spent hours travelling by train, back and forth along both lines, despite having nowhere to go. I'd alight at various stations and wander back and forth along the platforms before transferring to another train. In the company of many, yet paradoxically feeling alone. Something about the Metro felt comfortable and safe.

The Metro is more than a public transport network. It is an example of the new Leningrad. Every time I ride it, it is an example of the new me.

CHAPTER 31

January 5, 2022

ADAM

'You notice nobody who went to the club last night is here yet,' Louise said.

'They may have already had breakfast,' I said.

'On the way home?'

We were meeting in the hotel lobby at 9.30 this morning, which was comparatively late for this type of tour, but unlike many tours that try and rush through too many cities in a short time, there's a little bit more flexibility here. Still, it feels like an early start for those out most of the night. Louise and I were either restrained enough or just too old for it to be a problem.

The breakfast room was reasonably full, and when Lila walked in, she joined us, valuing the seat enough that she was willing to put up with my conversation.

'Good morning,' she said.

'Dobroye utro,' I replied, trying to make it look like my Russian was progressing as I repeated her greeting.

'You sound almost like a local.'

'Really,'

'No. Still, it always serves you well to say just a few words in the local language wherever you are. People appreciate the effort. Not getting it right is not disrespectful, but not making an effort can be seen that way.'

I always did, however poorly. Usually, the key phrase I made sure I knew in the local language was 'I don't speak the language,' but I was also sure to be able to greet and give thanks in the local language, even if that was my limit.

As usual, I continued quizzing Lila about local life. I'd seen President Putin on the television screen when we were coming downstairs, and I wondered how the impression of the locals differed from his profile internationally.

'We don't tend to talk about politics in these situations. Putin has been running this country since I was a child, so that is all I know. Right, wrong, it does not matter.'

'Does that not bother you?' I asked.

'It doesn't matter whether it does or not. It won't change anything. When you are in a situation you cannot change, you are better off accepting it and focusing on the things you can impact.'

'But are you free to say what you believe?'

She shrugged her shoulders. 'There are things I prefer not to find out.' She looked around the room momentarily and felt a level of safety to say a little more. 'You know, Putin is from Saint Petersburg. Some people admire someone who has grown up tough and made it to the top, while others maybe dislike someone who has forgotten where he came from.'

'And you are?' She cut me off before I finished.

'Not going to say anymore.' Sometimes, when a person says nothing, they say everything.

'There are much better things in Saint Petersburg to discuss than politics,' she said.

'Absolutely,' Louise said, sick of a topic that didn't interest her.

'What are you looking forward to today, Louise?'

'All of it,' she said, struggling to remember the day's agenda. 'How does the metro here compare with Moscow?'

'It's a much smaller network, though the highlights are similar,' she said.

As an optional part of the tour, we knew not everyone would be joining us on the Metro tour. Many would have questioned why touring several subway stations in such a beautiful city was worthwhile. Still, Saint Petersburg and Moscow have very different and memorable public transit networks.

When the Saint Petersburg Metro was established, Stalin encouraged the approach of Moscow's Metro to be followed, aiming to recreate the same principle established in the capital. The stations were designed to be far more than a place to catch a train. 'Palaces for the People' was the expression used. The regime's mindset was that the masses lived in standardised, uninteresting houses and then spent the rest of their time working repetitive and tedious jobs for their society. They needed inspiration to continue to get the best out of the masses, and that inspiration was to come on their daily commute. Getting on the train at one station, generally transferring at another, and then alighting at a third station, the opportunity to provide unique experiences at each station would maximise the benefit of this principle. The best minds were put to creating stations that represented the area or an element of Soviet life. Louise and I were blown away by how unique the stations of Moscow were, and if Saint Petersburg got remotely close to this, it was an unmissable attraction.

I think last night had written off a couple more, leaving ten of us joining Lila as we left the hotel just after 9.30. We walked in a different direction from all the previous times, heading south. After a couple of blocks, we'd reached the Fontanka River and soon passed yet another majestic-looking cathedral, which Lila called the Trinity Cathedral, despite its name in Cyrillic appearing to be a hundred letters long.

'Not everything translates perfectly between our languages,' she explained.

We were passing the Institute of Technology a couple of blocks past this, which was apt when the familiar-looking M symbol to signify the railway appeared, and we were at Tekhnologichesky Institut Station.

'We are starting our tour here at Tekhnologichesky Institut, despite the fact it is not the closest station to our hotel, but because it is not that much further, and it is on line 1, which is where so many of the best stations are,' Lila said.

The station was unusually set up. All the trains going south were in the hall we had entered, while all the trains going north ran to another hall. Typically, stations that serve two lines have different halls split by line rather than the direction of travel. The hall we were in was amongst the first of the Saint Petersburg Metro and was an elaborate tribute to Russian and Soviet science, in keeping with the institute above us. The hall is decorated in expensive marble and adorned with portraits of famous scientists. From the hall's centre, Lila gathered us in close and gave us a bit of history, stopping in the middle when the noise of an arriving train was too great for her to be heard over the top of.

'The Saint Petersburg Metro was planned before World War II, but construction had barely started when it was stopped for the war. It wasn't until 1955 that it opened. While it was modelled on the 'people's palace' concept used in Moscow, much of the network was only planned after the death of Stalin. When Khrushchev came to power, there were many policy changes. Whereas Stalin was focused on inspiring the workers, Khrushchev wanted the trains running with as little money spent as possible. As such, the planned initial stations of Line 1 are palatial, but the newer stations reflect the more practical approach that took over.

'We will be heading south on this line, catching the train and stopping at a few of the coming stations.'

There is little need for a train timetable here. Trains on each line run roughly every two minutes. Because of all the rivers and canals, the underground network here is the deepest in the world. As you go down the escalators from the station entry to the platforms, you will likely have a couple of trains arriving and departing. Knowing the next will be so close behind, there is little need to panic about missing a train. In the few minutes we've been downstairs, that hasn't been apparent, watching the locals sprint at the sight of a train.

We caught the first train two stops to Narvskaya. Originally, this station was named Stalinskaya, but when Khrushchev came to power, there was a push to 'de-Stalinise' as much as possible. In Moscow, we saw a station where Stalin had been airbrushed out of a mural. His name had gone here, but the tributes were still apparent. There is Stalin quote regarding the "glory of socialism" on an upstairs wall, and another quote, "Glory to Work," greets travellers as they descend the escalator.

Along the main hall are sculptures dedicated to various types of workers, artists, farmers, architects, textile workers, doctors and soldiers. All of those whom the successes of the Soviet state depended on were honoured, and this was meant to culminate in a bust of Stalin. There were symbols, such as red flags and the hammer and sickle, to retain the national tribute, just not the personification of these through the former leader.

The next station, Kirovskiy Zavod, was named for the nearby Kirov engineering plant, one of the world's largest industrial plants. For many, this would have been their morning destination, and they were to be inspired by a grey marble and a style of lighting that felt like natural daylight.

'They're not skylights?' one of the other travellers asked.

'No, but they are designed to look that way. If we were reliant on natural light in winter, it would be an issue here,' Lila explained. There was also the fact that the roof where these so-called skylights sat was 50 metres underground. A skylight at that depth wouldn't give much light in any conditions.

The next station was Avtovo, the station most synonymous with the Saint Petersburg Metro, considered one of the world's most beautiful subway stations. On the station's far wall is a mosaic celebrating victory in World War II with a woman holding a child. The station is just a few kilometres from the front line that the Nazis reached, and this station celebrates the people's will to overcome the horrors. The rows of glass and marble columns and the elegant chandeliers that light the main hall and the platform areas add to the majestic beauty and symbolise victory.

We crossed over to the other side of the station to get a train heading north, going beyond our point of origin. Our destination was Pushkinskaya. Built 150 years after the birth of Alexander Pushkin, this station was right by the above-ground station where trains ran to Tsarskoye Selo, the town where Pushkin spent much of his life. In more recent times, the town was renamed Pushkin in tribute. The station's main feature is a magnificent statue of the poet in front of a mural of the park in his home suburb, where another statue of Pushkin now sits.

Our next stop was our last on line 1, at Ploschad Vosstaniya, named after the square immediately above it. The name translates to Uprising Square, so named for its role in hosting numerous revolutionary protests and demonstrations in 1917. This was the first underground station opened in Saint Petersburg, and being right by the Moskovsky Station, where we arrived by train from Moscow, it is usually the first underground station travellers see. In keeping with its role in the evolution of the USSR, the Soviet Union flag features prominently, as does red granite to compliment the vast amount of marble throughout the station.

We transferred from here to Line 3 via a transfer corridor and an escalator. Although connected, we were now in Mayakovskaya station. Mayakovskaya was the name of one of the most beautiful and extravagant metro stations in Moscow, but in Saint Petersburg, it is an interesting yet very different-looking station. Named after Borislav Mayakovsky, a poet and Russian futurist, this station is red, covered in mosaics and incredibly bright. A decade newer than any of the stations we'd seen before this, it bore little resemblance to the stations on line 1, the Khrushchev influence obvious. However, it had a powerfully unique and eye-catching look and proved that there was more than one way to impress.

One station on, we arrived at the comparatively uninteresting Ploschad Alexandra Nevskogo station, where we alighted not to see the station but to change lines again. We moved to Line 4, walking a hundred metres to a significantly newer part of the station. This time, we travelled two stops to Dostoevskaya. Located just near his former apartment, now the Dostoevsky Museum, the station honours the author of such works as Crime and Punishment and The Demons.

One station further on was Spasskaya, a station connected to two others on different lines, and it was here that we transferred to Line 5. Although connected stations, this part was called Sadovaya, the same as the street name of our hotel. The station itself was right near the restaurant we ate at last night.

'We will get on the next train and travel one stop, which will end the tour,' Lila said.

Admiralteyskaya is one of the newest stations on the network, opened in 2011 and named after the nearby Admiralty Building, between the Bronze Horseman and Palace Square.

'This is the deepest station under Saint Petersburg,' Lila told us. 'It is so far below ground that it was impossible to use one escalator the whole way, so an 80-metre escalator takes you to an intermediate level before another takes you the rest of the way. Depending on where you're travelling, the escalator ride ends up longer than the train ride.'

CHAPTER 32

December 1975

EKATERINA

Over the previous few years, I had begun coming back to Pyshech-naya more regularly. I had enquired about the possibility of returning to work, not out of the need to be earning, but to justify my regular visits to the shop. There weren't any vacancies, but that was perhaps for the best. Rather than it being a place to come and serve others, it was a place I could come to for myself. I felt a degree of comfort whenever I walked in the door here, reconnecting me with the memories of Babushka and the wonderful early days of married life with Borislav.

Memories are strange; reminders of Borislav in many situations are inherently sad, as they always centre on the end, yet in Pyshechnaya, the memories always settle in the golden moments at the beginning of our marriage. Essentially, I feel a level of safety and contentment when I am here that keeps my mind from the discomforts that follow me everywhere else.

There is a great paradox to people for me. As much as possible, I seek to avoid people, craving the solitude that removes the discomforts that others provide. Despite that being my natural instinctive thought, there is an irony to the fact that the place I am most comfortable is this permanently busy doughnut shop where there is never the remotest possibility of solitude.

Now I come here every day. I get a couple of pyshki and a cup of coffee and spend a couple of hours here. I watch the people come and go, study them and think about their lives. In most cases, they're all the same. People don't have better or worse lives because the quality of life comes back to individual perceptions. The more pain you go through, the more conditioned you are to it, and the less impact a negative experience has on you. Similarly, the more charmed your life is, the less appreciation you have for each positive event. The simplicity of a peaceful morning in Pyshechnaya with my pyshki and coffee is divine for me, yet it is just a plain and ordinary occasion for most people I watch. They struggle to deal with the news of a minor inconvenience. I struggle to deal with the memories of losing every person I've ever loved. The good and the bad feelings are similar, even if the events that inspire these are markedly different.

I take note of most people when they walk in the door, but I usually pay more attention to them once they've stopped to eat. That wasn't the case when one particular woman walked in. Short blonde hair, about fifty, she would have been able to blend into most places, but in my eyes, she stood out like a beacon. She wasn't paying too much attention to anyone in the shop, focussing on finding a vacant table while her husband joined the queue.

'Anastasia,' I said as I approached her from the side.

She turned and looked at me, her face more filled with curiosity than any sense of happiness or relief.

'Ekaterina?'

'Yes, it is me.'

'I can't believe it. You survived.'

'And you. We thought you had perished.'

Her husband arrived at the table with a tray of pyshki and two cups of coffee. Anastasia introduced me to Andrei, and we began the lengthy explanations of what life had brought each of us over the past thirty years.

'Did you never look for us?' I asked, still disappointed by her decision to leave us all those years ago. I had lost every family member throughout my life, but other than Anastasia, they had all been through death. She alone had chosen to leave.

'I did what every sensible person in this city had done. I got out. I never came back until now, on holiday, using the opportunity to show my husband the city I grew up in.

'Although by some miracle you survived, I was constantly seeing death every day. The only hope I saw for life was escape. I didn't want to leave you and Dasha, but I had no time to think or plan when the opportunity arose. Immediate action was the only choice, and I hoped and prayed that left on your own, Dasha, and you would survive long enough until someone came along to take care of you. I couldn't. Obviously, my prayers were answered. What happened to Dasha?'

I explained the orphanage and the church shelters and told her I had never seen Dasha since we were split up into different churches.

'I always wanted to believe that her experiences were very different to mine. I'm sure my church was very much the exception, so things would have probably been better for her. What happened to her from that point on has been a mystery.'

'You didn't look for her?'

'Of course,' I said. 'When I left the church shelter, I didn't want to draw attention to myself, so I steered clear of anywhere official, but once I felt any possible heat would have died down, I went to the Nikolsky Cathedral and asked after her. Initially, they said they couldn't divulge any information, but a woman there felt sufficiently sympathetic that she told me what she knew. Unfortunately, that wasn't much. She had left the church as soon as she turned sixteen and gave no indication of where she was headed. Whether she stayed in Leningrad or moved on, I had no idea. I looked, but with no leads, it was little more than constantly keeping my eyes open wherever I was. The same way I've now found you. Maybe one day Dasha will walk through the door.'

As children, the dynamics between Anastasia, Dasha and myself were complicated. Anastasia had to grow up much faster than Dasha and I, taking a more adult role in the house as things became tougher during the Siege. It may have been Anastasia and Dasha who were sisters, though it seemed more like Dasha and I had that kind of relationship, even if the siblings shared the more volatile personality type.

Anastasia went to the bathroom, leaving Andrei and me to talk. He mentioned they had two children, both grown up, Damir and Tiana. He asked more about our home life as children, and I explained the dynamics of our household and the extended family that lived there in the quickest and simplest terms.

'How much has she ever talked about it?' I asked.

'Not in great detail, though I knew what had happened to most of the family.'

'Did she ever say that she had left while there were still some of us here?'

He paused, reflecting on conversations that surely would have been more common thirty years ago. She said that she and her mum had left the rest of the family for work, and when her mother died, she took the opportunity to go to Moscow. Whenever it had been mentioned about trying to find any of you, she said that none of you had survived.'

'She doesn't seem overly enthralled to find she was wrong.'

'People are enthralled when they've hung on to hope and have it realised. She had accepted your fate so long ago that finding you now is more confusing than exciting.'

Everyone is the product of their experiences. For me, life has been constant loss. For Anastasia, the first third of her life was the same, but ever since leaving Leningrad, she appears to have lost no one or nothing. Perhaps she has enough now that there is no need to value anyone else, whatever their history or blood ties. There may have been times in my life when I have pushed people away, but never those I was indelibly linked to.

She returned to the table and talked more about the doughnut shop, avoiding anything more in-depth. With time, I tried to turn the conversation back towards our lost loved ones, but with that, she seemed unwilling to engage too far.

'With everything that happened around us, our family was destined to be destroyed. It started with what happened to our fathers, and it followed through with the decision of the remaining adults to stay when the Siege started. I am sorry for all you have endured, but that is how it had to be.'

Her attitude towards me was similar to how it was in childhood. We were always a burden to her, and it seemed my presence was the same to her now. The shock of finding me after all these years had no impact. She was keen to move on and forget the discovery.

'I enjoyed hearing the story, and I am so grateful that you are one of the lucky ones who survived, but the Siege made new people out of all of us. Whether we stayed or left, it tore us apart and made us begin a new life. The girls we had been were cousins, but the women we were forced to become have nothing that links us. We all do what we need to survive, and for me, that meant leaving the past where it was.'

'Yet here you are, in Leningrad.'

'To remind myself and to show Andrei who I once was. It is not who I am. Goodbye, Ekaterina, and good luck.'

She got up from her seat and walked to the door, not even waiting for Andrei, who briefly stopped and apologised. He did say that he respected her wishes before chasing after her.

Half an hour ago, I was alone in the world. Contrary to all I thought I knew, I briefly got to suspend that thought at the realisation that my cousin had survived against all odds. As it turns out, she had proven to be the only person who had willingly chosen to remove me from her life. The pain of losing someone to tragedy has defined my life. Now, I have found a very different feeling inside when you lose someone through their choice. I don't know how to define it, but it lies somewhere between anger, resentment and a simple form of sadness.

I wonder if the same would apply if I ever did find Dasha. Today's experience makes me hope I don't find out. I've always retained the thought, or is it hope, that when she left the Nikolsky Cathedral, she found herself a new life, a job, a husband, had children and lived a content life. Without anything to prove otherwise, I will hang on to those thoughts. I don't think I want to lose them, and I feel like finding her is liable to have more potential downsides than upsides.

CHAPTER 33

January 5, 2022

ADAM

We'd had a very light lunch at a snack bar just around the corner from Saint Isaacs Square, just a short walk from Admiralteyskaya Station. Our bus met us near the cathedral for the rest of our day's activities, hopefully with the other half of our group having survived and now surfaced.

'Hey, how was your night?' I asked Ben and Nadia, the first two I saw when I boarded. The sunglasses on the gloomy day already told me enough.

'Good,' was Ben's quick and straightforward answer before Nadia offered more information, saying they'd visited about four more clubs. All had free entry, which made bar hopping more attractive.

'I think the scene is different in summer and on weekends. We saw it at its quietest, but still, it was a good night. How about you guys?'

'We pretty much went home when we left you.'

'Pretty much?' Louise said. 'He means, we did.'

Nikki laughed, knowing that without Louise's confirmation and understanding, I seemed to be suffering from a desire to believe I was younger than I was.

It was only a short bus ride over the Palace Bridge and along the Neva's bank until we reached another bridge, crossing onto the Peter and Paul Fortress. This tiny island was originally set up as a fortress to protect the yet-to-be-built city from a feared Swedish naval attack. The fort was never required as the Swedish were defeated before ever making it as far as Saint Petersburg, but once built, the fortress was destined to play a different role in the city's history. It served as a jail for many years, with Dostoevsky, Trotsky and Lenin's brother Alexander amongst the people incarcerated there.

The island's primary focus is the Peter and Paul Cathedral, yet another house of worship to add to yesterday's list. The oldest church in Saint Petersburg also has a higher point than anywhere in the downtown Saint Petersburg region because of its enormous spire. Topped with an angel weathervane, the tower appears to have inspired the design of the Admiralty building we saw yesterday.

Immediately upon walking inside, I was struck by how different the cathedral looked from the ones we saw yesterday. The chandeliers looked more reminiscent of the imperial palaces than most churches, but the reason soon became apparent. This cathedral was the burial place of every Russian emperor from Peter the Great onwards. Knowing the luxury they demanded, any thought of resting eternally somewhere would have seen them needing a similar style.

'You can see that the Peter and Paul Cathedral is far more like a Catholic cathedral than an Orthodox one. Fewer icons, more gold. There aren't the pews of a Catholic church, but there is a pulpit.'

Like all the churches we'd seen, it was far more a museum than a place of worship. The layout made it seem more of a memorial to the Romanov family than any form of honouring God. The religious elements appeared to serve more in the hope that the spirits would protect the deceased than to look out for those who came to pay their respects.

The graves themselves were all ornately decorated. At the front right was Peter's grave, freshly adorned with flowers from mourners. I wouldn't have thought too many people got that love close to three hundred years after death. A bust of Peter the Great is at the head of his tomb.

After finishing in the cathedral, we moved quickly around the rest of the island, but our time was limited, meaning we wouldn't get to see inside the other buildings. Of most note on the island was the Saint Petersburg Mint, founded in the city's early days and still operational. Almost every other part of the island was run by the State Museum of Saint Petersburg History.

We walked down a street that looked like a standard suburban street with houses on both sides, standardised in three categories for noblemen, the middle classes and the impoverished. Lila explained that Peter was a believer in standardised and simplified development. While looking at 18th-century development here is a world away from the 20th-century Soviet-style development across the city, the standard plans did have a connection.

Most of the buildings on the island now serve as specialist museums. The Trubetskoy Bastion Prison served this purpose, providing an insight into what the likes of Dostoevsky faced in their time here. Other buildings included a space museum, a city history museum, a science and technology museum and a history of money museum. Still, we didn't go into any of these on our tight schedule.

We passed a cannon that was fired each day at midday, reflecting the signal of the start and end of each workday on the island in the time of Peter the Great. We arrived too late to experience it today.

'We could come tomorrow,' Louise said, based on our lack of plans and several hours of free time between checkout and the bus to the airport.

'Maybe. But it is just a cannon,' I said.

We passed through the Gate of Peter the Great, the official entrance point to the island. From outside the gates, we had a supreme view across the river to the central part of the city.

Back inside the walls, we headed back to the bus and our movement onto the next stop. I wasn't sure whether we were headed back along the same pathway, as it had looked unfamiliar other than a sculpture of rabbits that I was sure I'd already seen.

'Lila, what's the story with all these sculptures of hares?' Louise asked, more confident that the one before us was different from what we'd already seen and seemingly more aware of the difference between hares and rabbits than I was.

'While we know this whole island now as Peter and Paul Fortress,' Lila said, 'the island is called Zayachy, which translates to Hare Island. It was called this due to a legend of a hare leaping into the boot of Peter the Great during a flood and being saved. There is one monument on a log in the water where there is a long-standing superstition. You make a wish as you throw a coin on the log where the hare stands. Your wish comes true if the coin lands and remains on the log. On the island, there are many more works by various sculptors.'

We came to a bizarre-looking monument so disproportionate that I was initially unsure if it was meant to be a tribute to anyone.

'This is a famous monument to Peter the Great,' Lila told us. 'It may look strange, but the head was made according to the after-death mask and is quite accurately sized, but the body was designed using the same dimensions as the icon painters always used. As a result, it looks like a baby's head on a giant's body. You will also notice the hands. They are incredibly shiny because it is a superstition, like we have seen with other statues here and in Moscow. With this one, rub Peter's hands and make a wish; it will come true.'

'It doesn't work. I tried that with the statue in Moscow, and I still ended up hungover on New Year's Day,' Cherie said.

'I make no guarantees on the effectiveness of our superstitions', Lila said before continuing with other details of the island's history. I moved away from the group, looking at the statue from a different angle. Johannes and Marizane approached me, only now catching up to the rest of the tour group. They were the only two smokers in our tour party, and there were many occasions when they would drift off from the group and only catch up to us as we were about to move on.

'Can you believe that's the same character we've seen in all these other depictions?' I said.

'Based on his head, I'd say he was 3 foot 2, based on his torso, 12 foot 10,' Johannes said.

'I guess everyone interprets everything through their view,' Marizane said. 'Same as the way things are reported on. How the world saw everything in South Africa 30 years ago was very different from how we saw it.'

'Nothing ever gets better,' Johannes added.

'You don't think?

'Definitely. It's like the laws of physics. Every action has an equal and opposite reaction. That dictates every aspect of our world. We had an oppressed majority, and when that changed, life was greatly improved for many, but for some, the losses were immeasurable.'

'Are you defending apartheid?' I asked.

'I'm not talking right and wrong, just the forces surrounding these things. You give me a ruble, and I take it. There is no change to the overall picture. You are worse off, and I am better off by the same amount.'

'If I give you a ruble that was not going to be used, and you spend it somewhere, it may lead to benefits passing through many people. The owner of the business, the employees, the places they spend the money, the government through tax,' I said. 'The benefits gained across society are far greater than my loss.'

'At the end of the day, you're still down one ruble. If 50 different people or groups have each gained, it's just a couple of kopeks each. It remains an equal and opposite force,' he argued. 'If everything is equal, ruthless people will always work on ensuring they win on each equation. Power and money buy more of the same.

'That's what drove old small-head here,' he said, pointing to the statue of Peter the Great. 'Leaders have operated that way throughout history, and today's leaders haven't changed. The only difference is the way these battles are fought. Russia would have invaded and conquered Ukraine in 2014 if the accountability of today was what it was in centuries gone by. They still might.'

While I didn't agree with all that he said, there was certainly merit to some of it. In Western democracies, our politicians were on a permanent war footing, not through preparing tanks and bombs, but through information and lies. If your public was exposed to a single narrative that you controlled, then anyone could be made out to be a significant threat to you and your country. The truth was irrelevant. The belief was what mattered. People don't believe the good you promise, but fear is an overriding emotion, and people always fear things that are threatened correctly.

It has been just over thirty years since the Soviet Union disbanded. Communicating all that was happening at that point was very different today. Now, the moment something happens, someone has tweeted it, and in moments, it is in front of the faces of millions. Whether it is true, the whole truth and nothing but the truth is rarely verified.

'You know,' Johannes added, 'ever since the term fake news was coined, truth has become irrelevant. If you don't agree with something, you discredit it with those two words. The footage is from a different time and place, or those statistics have been modified by including irrelevant data; there is always a way. And the people who share your views won't need proof of discrediting.'

I told him about the coup of 1991 and the playing of Swan Lake across all the TV channels.

'Before technology changed, you didn't need the term fake news. You could ensure people never saw the news. Maybe not in our countries, but right here in this city, that is what they did.'

CHAPTER 34

August 19, 1991

EKATERINA

I woke up this morning and put the television on. Every channel was screening Swan Lake. It was apparent that there had either been a significant death in the Kremlin or an overthrow of the government. The media had no freedom in covering this, but the screening of the ballet by all media outlets served as something of a code.

Eventually, there was a break in the transmission, and an announcement was made. The State Committee on the State of Emergency had launched a coup, and the government of Mikhail Gorbachev had effectively been overthrown. In our country, we cannot always rely on the media for truthful accounts of events but for delivering the message that those in charge want us to hear. The fact that we were hearing this suggested the plotters had succeeded.

There was incredible tension in the country as the reforms put into motion in 1989 were getting closer to completion. The Soviet Union would be no more, and the new Russia would be democratic, capitalistic and progressive. In our city, the name of Leningrad would be gone in just two more weeks, replaced by the former name of Saint Petersburg. A two-thirds majority vote for change had prevailed in the June referendum. Many of my generation were unhappy about this, yet I couldn't have been more optimistic about it.

Although the city carried Lenin's name, it was predominantly in the era of Stalin that the city became all it was known for. This had been a very different set of qualities than the city had been borne from at the turn of the eighteenth century. Peter had sought a city of culture, openness and freedom. The Soviet era was defined by isolation, authoritarianism and blandness. It wasn't a straight rejection of all that the Soviet era stood for, but for most in the city, we sought a return to the city of Peter, and the name change would best reflect this.

The issue of the name stirred controversy. Even the reforming President Gorbachev rejected the change. He urged people to retain the name Leningrad as a tribute to all those who lost their lives in the Siege. As someone who lost far too many people, I felt the better tribute was returning greatness to the city. That would be best done by returning Peter the Great's influence. A name is just a symbol, but a symbol of our greatness would achieve more than a symbol of our darkest era.

Most of our city's people saw the reforms coming as the beginning of a better life. Freedoms and opportunities that we'd yearned for started to seem likely to disappear before they arrived. The people behind the coup were the hard-liners from the Communist Party and the KGB. Their unwavering aim was to retain the USSR and its nature of operations, stopping and rewinding any reforms Gorbachev had initiated.

Curiosity got the better of me. I decided to go out and see what was happening. From my window, I'd been relieved to see little sign of the streets being overrun, but I decided to venture towards the Marinsky Palace, where the local council and our mayor, Anatoly Sobchak, were based. As a vital ally of the reformers, any attempt to overthrow Gorbachev would also be aimed at Sobchak and the local authorities.

I was surprised at how few people were out on the streets. There didn't seem to be any form of organisation that had taken control. I walked along the Moyka River embankment, and as I closed in on Saint Isaacs Square, there was no sign of the tanks I'd expected. The few of us wandering in town seemed keen to support those protesting the coup, but no such protest had emerged.

As the day marched on, the crowds grew. By midday, thousands in Saint Isaacs Square were holding up hastily made banners showing their support for the government. After spending decades hiding the majesty of this city in the name of the Soviet regime, we had just started to see the rebirth of freedom and positivity, and nobody wanted to lose that. Well, not nobody.

A man not too much older than me was there wearing his war medals and ranting about the government destroying the country he loves and the country he fought for, the Soviet Union. Many of his age group shared a similar stance, though few publicly displayed these feelings. For someone born a generation before me, the October Revolution stood in the same part of their memory as the Siege of Leningrad sits in mine. Those recollections may be imperfect, but they shape attitudes from such a formative part of life. With the spirit of the Bolsheviks, these small minorities were passionate in their pleas, but they were massively outnumbered by those of us who yearned for the soon-to-be-renamed Saint Petersburg to return to the vision of Peter the Great.

There was little reason for me to feel so invested in everything that was happening. Life at this point offered little difference to me, whatever the political circumstances were. I was middle-aged and alone, with no need to worry about a future legacy. I didn't work. I lived off a small part-pension and long-term savings from inheritance and insurance. What was the difference to me? I understood that I didn't matter. What was good for the city and the country was what mattered. People like me could adjust accordingly, but as a society, we needed to do what was right for the masses. It seemed certain to me that we needed to harness the spirit that originally fuelled this city. We needed to be Saint Petersburg, not just by name, but in the essence of what that name represented.

One of the things that I didn't do today was bring my camera. It has become a significant part of my life again over the past couple of years, for the first time since Borislav was alive.

Art is integral to what defines the true Saint Petersburg that we want the city to become again. This city was the home of ballet, the home of the world's greatest art museum, and the home of some of the greatest writers and composers in history. My artistic expertise may be limited, but I was passionate about photography when I first met Borislav, so I decided to rekindle that passion. For far too long, life had consisted of too little, and for a person with so many bad memories, the only sensible approach to life was to be busy moving forward with new passions rather than remaining tied to the past.

The most beautiful city in the world. Naturally, this title cannot be given definitively to any city. If you ask a hundred different people, you will get dozens of different answers, but no doubt several will answer Saint Petersburg. The city's story and the history's impact add to what is on offer, but the actual beauty lies in the visual. For a photographer, few places on earth offer the opportunities here.

Every day, I would find a different part of the city to focus on. I would either make my way out early or spend my morning at Pyshechnaya before photographing. I never overthought what I intended to achieve from this work, but having something to work on gave me a reason to look forward to each day. I would often return to locations I'd shot previously, looking at weaknesses in my work and trying to create better results.

I still felt uncomfortable around people, meaning most of my work was built around landscapes and buildings, but I wanted to photograph people, too. I felt photography could be an ideal way of telling people's stories, so I began to feature them in photos, albeit as minor details against spectacular backdrops rather than the focus.

The closest I got to trouble with the camera was near the epicentre of today's action at Saint Isaac's Square. I had been set up in the middle of the Konnogvardeyskiy Bul'var, a park that separates the two sides of the main road between Saint Isaacs Square and the Naval Museum. I was trying to capture some of the office workers coming out of the gas works headquarters with some of the formality of their look against the casual touristy look familiar in this part of town. Unfortunately, some more formally dressed types weren't impressed with the idea of being caught on film.

'Who are you?' A couple of threatening people, who I suspected were far more than gas company employees, asked me.

I wasn't likely to be a significant threat at my age, but the end of the Soviet era had not seen a change in the secret services' approach here. There was no innocent until proven guilty attitude from them. If they doubted you, there was trouble.

I explained the type of photos I had been trying to take, apologised if I had inadvertently got them in my pictures, and offered to give them my role of film. They checked my identification, took my details and, most surprisingly, allowed me to go. They took the roll of film, but I knew I had little of value on it. More importantly, it was a lesson. People presented a whole other danger, and it was far better to ensure my creations were based on the city's majesty than the potential issues from its people. Perhaps there would be no issue most often, but as I learnt in childhood, you never knew when one person would threaten everything.

If ever there was to be danger from people, it was in the midst of a coup, though in the streets of our city, this was no ordinary coup. Police surrounded the square but took no action against anyone, for there was no conviction in who they were responsible for in light of the upheaval.

The following day, the crowds were larger after Sobchak had called for a public rally in Palace Square. Again, I left the camera at home, but made my way to be part of the masses. Three hundred thousand people packed the square, with tens of thousands in adjacent streets. Placards and banners were waved with slogans demanding an end to the coup, with dissent from the protesters appearing non-existent. The one moment of fear came mid-morning when movement arose in the Guards' Headquarters. What was the military preparing to do? I felt sure they couldn't take any drastic action against us. I was more than proven right when the soldiers released a hand-painted banner that read, 'We are with you.'

Sobchak spoke, and when he mentioned the city, he called it Saint Petersburg. As the rally continued, everyone shared an overriding feeling. The coup had fallen apart, and rather than bring an end to the direction of freedom, it had done nothing more than speed up the process. Our hero city was ready for the next stage of its history. Saint Petersburg was prepared to begin a new era, one that earned a reputation based on the beauty of today rather than the tragedy of the past. The mood throughout the square was one of celebration. All the news from Moscow had indicated that the coup was about to end.

The group of eight men who had led the coup, ranging from the vice-president of the Soviet Union to a range of other high-ranking officials within the government, the unions and the KGB, were all arrested. One committed suicide the following day, and the remaining seven were arrested to end their terms in public life. In the following days, several former Soviet republics declared independence, and by the end of the year, the Soviet Union was confined to history.

Two weeks after the coup, we were again celebrating on the city streets, but for the first time in three-quarters of a century, we were doing this on the streets of Saint Petersburg. The name of Leningrad was still used by all those who retained their support of all that the communist party had delivered since the time of the Bolsheviks. Officially, and in the eyes and words of most, Saint Petersburg, the most beautiful city in the world, was back.

CHAPTER 35

January 5, 2022

ADAM

Leaving the fortress, we were headed for a quick bus tour of some other islands that form part of Saint Petersburg, including Vasilevskiy and Krestovskiy.

The Spit of Vasilevskiy Island was one of the most popular spots for tourists to visit when they were in Saint Petersburg. The tiny car park was insufficient to accommodate all the cars and buses bringing people for a quick look at the spot. The area used to be the city's commercial port, and the prominent structures around the area reflect that. A customs house, warehouses and, most prominently, the Old Saint Petersburg Stock Exchange dominated the landscape. The stock exchange building looked more like a Greek temple than anything we'd seen in Russia. When the revolution led to a communist state, the building was no longer of use in its current form and was converted into a museum; this one focused on naval history.

Across the main road, a park formed an arrow to the water, with two large red rostrums at each end. These served as lighthouses to help direct ships as they approached the shore. We stopped first at the base of one of the rostrums.

More than anything, this area was the perfect photo opportunity, on the banks of the Neva with the city skyline, most notably the Winter Palace and the golden dome of Saint Isaacs standing out.

'If we were here on the weekend, trust me, you would have a dozen different couples in their wedding outfits jostling for the perfect position for that shot that will be on their mantlepiece for the rest of their lives,' Lila said. 'See that large granite ball over there? That is another local superstition. Smash your glass against the ball, and you will have good luck and a long-lasting marriage.'

'Nothing says good luck like broken glass,' I said, with a quizzical look to show what I thought of all these local superstitions.

Noticing Johannes and Marizane moving to the left to light up, I intentionally headed in the opposite direction. They were engaging in their own way. They did get me thinking and looking at things from a different perspective, but I found some of their attitudes disturbing. I'd had my fill of them for the day and wanted to enjoy this piece of the city without delving too deeply into the macabre.

'Come over here, Louise. Let's get some shots from down there where you can see the best backgrounds.' I was walking on the promenade that ran in a semi-circle by the river and between the rostral columns. From the first of these, we had an ideal view of the city centre, while as we walked around, Louise got a perfect photo of the fortress and the cathedral's spire.

We made our way through the park back to the first column, the designated meeting point for our group. We were quicker than some, but after making the group wait for me once in Moscow, I was determined not to be last again.

Back on the bus, we headed along the Neva edge as Lila commented on various sites as we passed. First was the Kunstkamera, the first museum ever opened in Russia. I learnt then that kunst was German for art when visiting the Kunstmuseum in Stuttgart. It was easy to look back at World War II and forget the links between Germany and Russia, but despite the different scripts used, it sometimes showed up in language.

The following highlights we passed were on the opposite side. Lila pointed out a sculpture on the embankment of a book, opened at a page from Pushkin's poem, The Bronze Horseman. This was immediately across the river from where the Bronze Horseman statue stands.

Further along, there were two museums on the river, one in the S-189 submarine and the next in the icebreaker Krasnin.

'Maybe we should come this way tomorrow,' I said to Louise.

Lila explained that these tours were all in Russian, so while we might be interested in what we saw, we mightn't learn much from it. I decided to keep it on our list of options, even if it wasn't at the top.

We turned off the embankment road to get a different perspective of the island. Soon after, we passed Erarta, a large modern art museum. Further into the island, the dominant feature was the rows of Soviet-era apartment buildings. While the city centre is filled with apartment buildings, they do not accommodate the masses like these. As a tourist, you often see the city without feeling it the way you do when you experience the suburbs and the backstreets. Even when we ventured out to the Imperial Palaces, we took the main roads that bypassed the real essence of life for the locals. While the metro gave us a taste, working through these parts gave us the best exposure to what life here was like.

One of the group asked Lila if she lived in this area.

'I grew up around here, and my parents still live here, but I have lived across town in the Kirovskiy district for many years. It is very similar. The residential areas right across the city are like this. It is the same in Moscow. The parts of the two cities seen in tourist mode make them seem like very opposite cities, but residentially, they are very similar.'

'I thought you said the cities were quite opposite,' Johannes said from his seat near the front.

'They are opposite from a cultural and lifestyle perspective,' she explained, 'but it doesn't mean there are no similarities. They are Europe's two most densely populated cities. Although I haven't been there, you would see similarities with New York or Hong Kong, where most people live tightly locked into high-rise apartments. If our cities had the type of housing of most European, American or Australian cities, they would sprawl out many times further.'

We came to a bridge, and she pointed out on the left, the Lakhta Centre.

'The Lakhta Centre is the tallest skyscraper, not just in Saint Petersburg, but all of Europe. Originally, they wanted to build a skyscraper in the city centre, but that motion was denied, as the city is a World Heritage site, and it was deemed that the building would affect the cityscape. A new plan was created to build an even taller structure out here. We will get closer soon, but in the meantime, we are about to move on to Krestovskiy Island, and the first feature you will see on the right is Gazprom Arena. This is the home of Zenit Saint Petersburg and played host to many of the key matches in the 2018 World Cup.'

This highway had no exit on Krestovskiy Island, and soon we were across onto the main part of northern Saint Petersburg. We were driven west to the Lakhta Centre and given additional information about it. I had hoped we would go to the observation deck to get the spectacular views of the city it would have offered. Lila gave us the disappointing news that it wasn't yet open, and we'd have to come back to the city again one day to experience that.

'This is not the furthest edge of the city, but you can see that further west, there isn't the same level of urbanisation for more than a kilometre or two. We are only ten kilometres from the centre of the city. In many other cities, this would still be almost called inner-suburban.'

The bus let us out near Piterland, a significant development that combined a shopping mall, a waterpark and various other adventure activities. This was not the purpose of our stop but rather a nearby footbridge that led across to Krestovskiy Island.

'This island is a combination of the where the city's top-end sporting talent compete and where the top end of town chooses to live.'

In addition to the futuristic football stadium with its retractable roof, there was an indoor velodrome and a multi-function indoor stadium for tennis, basketball, and handball. Across the island, there were also several tennis, rowing and yacht clubs, as the area dominated the sporting landscape of Saint Petersburg.

'How do you get onto the island?' I asked. There was no entry or exit to the island from the freeway when we passed over, and I assume that's why we had to walk on the footbridge.'

'There are bridges here, but the island's west end has no way on. It was quicker to walk and see part of the island and then meet our driver when he circumnavigates around to us just across the park,' Lila said. 'We will see just a little bit of how the favoured few live in this city. Housing that may seem more familiar to you but looks very different to the average Russian.'

Pobedy Park, the biggest public park in Saint Petersburg, dominated the middle section of the island, splitting the main sporting precinct in the west with the main residential area in the east. We walked through the central section and, once arriving at the main fountain, turned left, eventually meeting up with our driver. He had driven 25 kilometres to get to the point that we'd reached with a walk of one-tenth of that distance.

We took a roundabout journey along the island, seeing the first examples of upmarket housing I had seen in Russia. Of course, we had seen many palaces, but it had seemed like there was nothing for those between tsar and commoner. Modern Russia was home to vast numbers of very wealthy people, so it made sense that pockets of wealth had to exist. Krestovskiy Island was a reminder that there was a nobility close enough to the sources of power who demanded something more. It didn't matter what changes occurred across society and in the manner of government; there would always be haves and have-nots. Looking at this suburb, I wondered if it had ever been any different, whether it was in the times of the tsars, the Soviet era, or modern-day Russia under Putin.

We stopped at the end of a small street that intersected with what seemed to be a bustling road and inevitably faced a long wait. Looking out the window, I saw a playground that reminded me of the small park across the street from my home, half a world away in Adelaide. An old man pushed a small child on the swing while another couple of kids were at either end of the adjacent see-saw. For all the differences among us, there is nothing like innocent children at play to remind us that our similarities are far more significant.

CHAPTER 36

June 2006

EKATERINA

'There is nothing like the innocence of children, is there?'

The man hadn't noticed my presence before I began talking and continued to keep his focus on his grandchildren playing on the swings as he replied, having just briefly glanced at me. He had seen nothing more than a standard old lonely woman looking to make conversation, which he seemed keen to avoid.

'Easier retained now than in our day,' he said.

I moved a bit closer to him. The best part of a lifetime has passed, but the most distinct memories stay burned within us. I was not mistaken. I knew who this was.

'Who do you think I should tell? The children? Your family? The police? What do you think, Igor?'

He turned and faced me with a look of horror.

'Who are you?'

The fact that he was so horrified despite not knowing who I was disturbed me. To not immediately remember me implied that there had been too many other girls who he had inflicted the same type of atrocities on.

'Ekaterina Komarova was my name back then. 1948. The Church of the Resurrection.

His head dropped. He would have known there was no way the legal system would come after him after all this time, but that didn't remove all the threats I carried. He could counter with denial if I told these children or the rest of his family of the monster he had been, but it connects closely enough to the stories about that era in this city. When mud is slung, some always sticks, so there was no doubt he preferred to talk with me in confidence.

He called to the children and told them to keep playing while he sat down to chat with someone he had known as a child. I didn't appreciate his use of the word child, for there was nothing childlike about my recollections of him, whatever age he had been.

'I know nothing I can say will undo the damage, but I promise you the memories are as horrific for me as they are for you.'

'I sincerely doubt that.'

'Everything we did, we were compelled to do. Those priests, Ivanovich and Konstantin, were deviates. Whatever you experienced, their main focus was always on the boys. They raped us repeatedly and did this as training for us so that we would be as brutal with you girls. Their attacks on us partially groomed us to be the same sort of predators they were. I feel sick and disgusted at what I endured from them and what I put you girls through.'

How could I know whether these were the words of a man trying to mitigate his guilt or whether they were an accurate reflection? I never doubted that the priests were aware of the boys abusing us and were unconcerned by it, but it adds an extra element if the boys, too, had been victims.

'What about Vasilyevna?' I asked.

'We were told to kill her. We could only get someone new into the parish when a space became available. That happened when someone left, but the only way she would go would be by saying what had happened and risking what they had. So, they decided to have her killed. Naturally, they wouldn't do it themselves and made their trained predators do it.

'Yakov and I had an eight-hour window to kill her and dispose of the body. We didn't do it. We took her to the train station. I'm not proud of this, but we mugged a man on the way. We got more than we'd hoped from his wallet, funding a ticket for Vasilyevna to Moscow and 50 rubles to help her once she arrived.'

'If the two of you were the victims of such violent abuse, why didn't you take the money and run for it when you had that chance?' I asked.

'The man's wallet had nearly 200 rubles, so we also looked after ourselves. We figured you would be next, and we'd be doing the same for you. We wanted to protect ourselves, of course, but we also wanted to right some of the wrongs for you girls, too. But then, of course, you beat us to it.'

I had fled in mid-morning, my few possessions in a small bag, and I would have had no more than an hour away before the alarm would have been raised. I didn't have anywhere to go, but in 1948 Leningrad, a teenager on the street with nothing, was so inconspicuously common that I wouldn't create attention. I had no money to get a train, so I just started walking, without knowing where I would find myself. Similarly, the priests had no idea where to find me, so they inevitably gave up quickly.

'Their main method of finding you was through using Yakov and me. We were trusted after they believed in what we'd done to Vasilyevna, so it was believed we'd find you. If we did, we'd have got you out of the city to safety, but we had no success. A week later, we did the same as you. We left under the cover of night, but we went to Moscow. Before we went to the station, we stopped at the Nikolsky Cathedral and left a letter outlining everything the priests had done.'

'My cousin was living there,' I exclaimed, thinking of this as the closest reference I'd had to finding her in half a century. It was of little value, though, for Igor stressed that he'd merely dropped a letter there and seen nobody.

'When we were in Moscow, we sought guidance from a priest at a church down there. We explained everything that had happened, and he contacted the relevant authorities within the church. Ivanovich and Konstantin were arrested soon after. I never found out what happened, but our priest Alexei implied they'd never be seen in the outside world again. I chose to believe they'd been dealt with suitably. Sometimes what we believe to be true is more important than the actual truth.'

It was confusing hearing all of this after nearly six decades. Could anyone make this story up so quickly? He seemed to be recounting his version of the truth.

'Why did you never report them or us?' he asked.

'The past had taken everything I'd ever had. I could only afford to live in the future. I couldn't gain anything by chasing the perpetrators, so why relive the horrors? The aim was to move on and find a better life.'

'Yet here you are.'

'I never looked for you, but when by chance I found you, it seemed destiny was demanding that I have this conversation.'

'Maybe you're at a point in life now where it is of more benefit to know the whole story than just the part you were exposed to,' he said.

He told me more details about his life. After the news about the priests came through, he moved back to Leningrad and got a factory job. Soon after, he was married and had three children. That he was now in upmarket Krestovskiy Island seemed surprising, though my presence here would seem equally unusual.

'It was like a new life began when I returned to Leningrad. I did go past the church and found it abandoned. The horrors were great enough that they didn't bring anyone new to reform things. I believe the truth never came out publicly, but no doubt some former residents would have known why that happened.'

'Did you ever find out what happened to Vasilyevna?'

'Of course. We went to Moscow to find her, and part of why I returned was because we succeeded. Yakov was madly in love with her. He was the father of the child she was pregnant with when she left. She had that child, and they married a couple of years later. I barely ever heard from them again, so I don't know if they're still with us, but at least all your fears for her were unfounded.'

It seemed incomprehensible that a girl could fall in love with someone abusing her, but I can never know if her experiences were quite like mine. The priests watched the boys attack me, and I know she said the same had happened to her. She always told me that the boys were only doing as was demanded of them, but I'd never made sense of it. I do remember looking in their eyes. Igor's looked empty, like a person without a soul, but Yakov looked like a sorry little boy with everything he did.

People in this city had done unspeakable things. There were many cases where this reflected who they were, and Priests Ivanovich and Konstantin were prime examples. Far more common were those who didn't have the same choice. Igor stated that he was one of these, and it seemed from everything that he had said to be true. Like the cannibals during the Siege, people can live with themselves after committing the most atrocious act if their only alternative is not to live at all.

The White Nights festival was in full swing. The city had changed so much in fifteen years since the name of Leningrad was confined to history. In this city's cultural and natural wonderland, this conversation with Igor was about an altogether different world.

Igor asked me about my life since then. I mentioned the tragedies of Borislav and Yevgeny but tried to remain focused on the positive elements of life.

'What a rich and full life it has been,' I said. In spite of everything, I truly believed it.

CHAPTER 37

January 5, 2022

ADAM

Everyone has their own ideas of what to expect from any foreign country. Regarding food and drink, there are some countries where everyone tends to have the same thoughts, and everyone I know hears Russia and thinks of vodka. I don't think we've had a meal that hasn't started with vodka, at least excluding our novelty experience in Moscow of lunch under the golden arches. With vodka being such an omnipresent part of life in this country, it is natural that there is a Vodka Museum, our next stop.

We were back at Saint Isaacs Square, the bus letting us out here as one of the few accessible spots to stop around these parts. We walked towards the direction of the Neva, and at the edge of the square was the Central Exhibition Hall. Established initially as stables and a horse guards riding school, but from the front, the building looks similar to the old Stock Exchange building we saw earlier on the Spit of Vasilevskiy Island with its prominent pillars. There are two prominent statues of rearing horses with naked statues of pagan gods alongside them. There were also statues on the top of the classical building.

Past the most impressive-looking stables imaginable, as they had previously been, we were now at Konnogvardeyskiy Bulvar, which Lila translated as Horse Guards Boulevard. This picturesque street had a park, more than a median strip, separating the two directions of travel.

At the beginning of this street were two six-metre columns of glory. Atop each of these columns was a statue, copies of statues at different spots in Berlin.

We walked through the centre section of the road, along a pathway between two tree-filled sections. Lila pointed out the buildings on each side, which seemed to house various businesses. While one of the main offices of the gas company was on our right, the left-hand side seemed far more tourist-oriented, with a souvenir shop, bar and restaurant among the operations. Just past these, we moved to the side of the road and crossed over, right out of the front of the Museum of Russian Vodka.

Lila spoke with a woman she introduced as Maria, our guide for the museum. Jeremy and the other young men were ready to pay attention. Maria looked like Anna Kournikova. At my age, the impact of such an appearance isn't quite the same, and after making that initial assessment, I only paid attention to her as long as the topics remained interesting. I wasn't sure how long the history of vodka could be that way.

Unlike the 500 rooms of the Hermitage, the Museum of Russian Vodka had just two. The first was filled with 24 exhibits, ranging from an overview of the grains used in its manufacture to the laws and the drinking habits dating back to Ivan the Terrible's reign. The most interesting exhibits for me were the old shot glasses and decanters on display. After taking in so much of the city's history in the past few days, I wondered whose hands these had all been in across the years.

Naturally, Peter the Great made an appearance before too long. Not that they would say it here, such is the reverence he is held in, but historical accounts suggest he could have been called Peter the Drunk, such was his reputation for consuming enormous amounts of alcohol. When he organised the events, he introduced penalties for certain misdemeanours, such as late arrival. This was often a penalty drink. Forget a shot of vodka. This was a massive glass that they'd have to down. While some of us wouldn't see this as much of a penalty, having the tsar hold you down until you sculled a huge and potent drink might not be ideal.

The next bit of history that surprised me was that a level of prohibition was introduced in Russia earlier than in the United States. Retail sale of alcohol was banned at the start of the war under the guise of avoiding having drunken soldiers. Liquor could be sold in restaurants, but consumption in such circumstances was massively reduced. The ban lasted for a similar length as in America, ending in 1925. Under Mikhail Gorbachev, in 1985, a new dry law was initiated. It didn't ban alcohol but restricted the amounts that could be bought and the times it could be sold. Massive taxes were also added to make it much more expensive. Drinking in public was strictly banned, and those caught were prosecuted. Vodka went from being a standard daily staple to a rare luxury. While consumption dropped and health improved, the economy suffered. Those who drank did so from black market purchasing, and the government saw none of the benefits. Just a couple of years later, this policy was repealed, and the traditional omnipresence of vodka began to re-emerge.

Maria left us as we moved into the next room, which we were all looking forward to. It was time to taste test, though this didn't work quite the same way as a wine taste test, with just a tiny sip of a wide array of wines. We each had three standard varieties to try, and each was served in a typically large Russian shot glass. The bar in the room meant that if you were particularly keen, you could pay to try any of the hundred or more available varieties. I figured those three decent vodkas well before dinner would be enough for me.

The shots were served with snacks, and we were told this was how Russians had their vodka. If not at the start of a meal, it would be served with particular snacks eaten as soon as the vodka was consumed. The snacks were a pickle, dark bread topped with mustard and pork lard. None of these looked particularly appealing to me.

'In the Soviet era,' Lila explained, 'bars were very simplistic, but one thing that was always present was that when you bought a vodka, you got one of these snacks served with it always, just to make sure that you don't get too drunk, too fast.'

Lila had been waiting in here while we'd had the half-hour tour of the history side of the museum. I wondered how many she'd downed in that time, though I suspected she may be better equipped than me to deal with it.

'I didn't expect you even to go that far,' Louise said after I willingly ate a pickle for the first time in my life, following the first of the vodkas. I knew she'd be happy to finish it for me, but I must admit that post-vodka, it wasn't as bad as I had expected.

The second vodka was incredibly smooth, and I felt even less inclined to chase it down with a snack, but I tried the egg, fish and onion combination. Again, it did little for me, and I needed a bite to feel like I'd done my bit.

The third glass didn't look like vodka as I knew it, but it was ginger-infused and darker. The smell impressed me, though we had been told not to smell or sip, just shoot. When I did, I was less enthused by the taste of it. This time, I went to the snack with more enthusiasm. However unappetising the pig lard sounded, I scoffed happily at that moment.

Louise drinks vodka more than me, though rarely straight. While she liked the first two, she hated ginger and wouldn't touch the third. Fortunately, Cherie had started at the other end and willingly swapped the original with Louise's ginger-infused vodka, and they were both happy.

I was unsure whether to go to the bar or not. I wanted a beer to wash down all these tastes, but I doubted the vodka museum went beyond vodka. Harry was already there, so I made my way up to gauge the bar and see if he was motivated by my thoughts.

'Let me guess, vodka, vodka or vodka?'

'I think so,' Harry said. 'I'm choosing vodka.'

'I think I'll wait until we get back to the hotel and let the homesickness take over and allow myself a beer instead.'

'I don't believe you're homesick, though I can believe the yearning for a beer.'

'You've got me worked out well,' I said.

I wouldn't want to live elsewhere, but I've never felt homesick overseas. I love leaving. I dread returning. In both cases, it is only due to what those two things symbolise. When you go, you are on an adventure. During your time away, there are new places, people, new experiences, and new lessons every day. When you go home, it immediately returns to routine, consistency and repetition. Even with the greatest routines to be repeating, returning to them always feels disappointing. It takes a few days before I'm happy to be home because, at the initial point of return, it feels sad to know the magical experience of the trip is over.

Despite my lack of enthusiasm for it, Harry had interpreted my appearance at the bar as a desire for another vodka, so he had bought me one. I did the right thing and downed it and the bread and pig lard it was served with.

'Now I'll stop until it's beer at the hotel,' Harry said, much to my relief.

On the bus back to the hotel, Lila made dinner suggestions but advised us all that this was the official end of the tour. Once we were off the bus, there was no guarantee we'd see any of these people other than Lila again. She would be in the lobby through the morning tomorrow for a final goodbye and for the exchange of documentation that was required.

Roughly half of the group, including Johannes and Marizanne, gave each other quick goodbyes and best wishes and headed upstairs to their rooms. The rest of us headed into the hotel bar and took over a few tables. I finally got my long-craved beer, and we sat with Harry and Judy at one of these tables, working out what we should do for dinner with the others. They and their children were flying to Newcastle via Heathrow in the morning and would be on the way to Pulkovo Airport before Louise and I would be awake, so tonight would be the last we'd see them. We agreed to go to the restaurant next door, and another half-dozen of the group joined us.

'You know, it isn't the only factor in our travel choices, but we always seek places the most different to what we know,' Harry told me after finishing our main meals. 'Through Africa, Asia, and the Middle East, we've had such incredible diversity of experience. I wish we'd had time to see some of the more remote parts of Russia, but there's still enough in the lifestyles here to see a very different view of life. Still, the same thing resonates more than anything else.

'What's that?' I asked.

'As much as we are all different, we are also all the same. We all want the best for ourselves and our families. We do what we can to make the best of today while building for a better tomorrow. How we do that may differ, but the goal is the same.'

The outside perception of Russia is far different from what you see here. Society may work differently, and for that, I think of home with the utmost appreciation for the mechanics of our society. We may see the constant failings of our governments at all levels and yearn for something better, but we can feel blessed that our system prevents the level of problems that can be driven by a rogue individual in the systems here. From the excesses of the tsars to the brutality of the early Soviet regime and the dangerous direction that seems to be accelerating today, the country is vulnerable. Not to the outside world but to the power-wielding people within the country. All of that is not a reflection of the average person in the street. That person is no different to the average person anywhere else.

I didn't want to be saying goodbye to these people. Although it took a few days into the trip to start bonding with our fellow travellers, it was sad to see things end once those bonds were built. Another day or week would be irrelevant, as the end would still be sad. Once we were back in the hotel bar, the numbers soon dwindled, with several of the group having 4:30 a.m. wake-up calls for their early morning bus to Pulkovo. Cherie and Jeremy were the only two left with us, and we decided to leave them alone, sensing they might be ready to build a different kind of bond.

Even though we were moving on to the next stage of our adventure in Finland, the end of this tour had me reflecting on what made each day of our time in Russia unique and special. I always plan to take that attitude home with me. I want to value every day.

CHAPTER 38

July 2015

EKATERINA

I value every day. However repetitive and mundane my life may look to others, I find something magical every day. Today, my trip to the doctor may be more unpalatable, but when I write in my diary tonight, there will again be something unique to mention. When I reflect at the end of the week, the month and on occasions from year to year, the words I write each night prove the importance of every single day.

'Very few people born here as far back as you are still with us. Eighty-one years is a great triumph, Ekaterina,' Dr Shvidkovsky said.

I didn't need to be told this. It was a triumph to get to eighteen, let alone eighty-one, with the circumstances I faced in life. He had misjudged me in thinking he needed to prepare me for any bad news with such talk. Bad news was always part of life, and I was ready for it. As it turns out, there was little definitive to tell me. Tests had shown that I had significant coronary heart disease, but there was no final view on what impact that would have. The condition would be fatal, but there was no timeline for this.

'Six months or six years, we cannot say with certainty. We also cannot do anything to prevent it. There is a surgical option, but the risks associated are very high. Considering the period of recovery and the likely increase to your lifespan, such an option is not worthwhile.'

How ironic that this was found now. Fifty-five years ago, my son was born with an aortic aneurysm. There was every probability that I had the same condition at birth, just a far milder version that has taken decades to become severe enough to be a concern.

Realistically, I considered the diagnosis to be good news. He indicated that my most likely cause of death was a burst aorta and a swift end. I didn't want to suffer for an extended period with a disease that would slowly wear me down. This would be something that would offer little warning, little suffering, just a quick finish to a long life. Barring a sudden discovery of immortality, that sounded like the best to be hoped for.

I hadn't needed to be told that my time was nearly up to know it, yet when you are given the words from a medical professional, it tends to put your focus on it far more. It wouldn't change my life, but it made me more conscious that I couldn't wait for anything I wanted to do.

My life was sufficiently simple that there was little I needed to consider. I'd never left the city, and I didn't want to. All that did feel like it was missing, other than the things that couldn't be controlled, was the knowledge of the whereabouts of Dasha.

It was nearly seventy years since I said goodbye to her as she left the orphanage. When I had freedom, I hoped to find her, but tracking people in this city was impossible in those days. My focus swiftly shifted to the future, and my thoughts of Dasha became less of a priority. As much as I retained hope, I never expected to see her again.

In recent years, everything began to seem possible. After finding Igor, he told me about Vasilyevna and Yakov. With some assistance from my friend Yuri, he was able to track down their details. Unfortunately, I didn't find what I had hoped for; both of them were deceased, though at least I found that they had lives that extended far beyond the dread of their youth. Years earlier, I had seen for myself the life Anastasia had found for herself, and though I don't know anything after our rendezvous forty years ago, I saw enough then to see she had a genuine chance at life. Dasha was the one mystery.

'Everyone leaves a trail,' Yuri had told me. Unfortunately, the trail people left at the end of World War II differed significantly from the clarity of the trail they leave today. When I left the Church of the Resurrection, the people I had escaped would have been determined to find me for their self-interest. Once that time passed, I don't think anyone has ever looked for me since. Perhaps Dasha searched as I did for her, but with similar results. Yuri maintained that those who were untraceable then can often be found now. I placed my hopes in his ability to track her, though my expectations remained grounded.

'Belyakova,' I reminded him. 'Dasha Belyakova. Born in 1932, she was last known to be living at the Nikolsky Cathedral. She left there in 1948, though nothing is known from then on.'

Despite initially making it sound like a simple task, Yuri admitted that it was a long shot that he could find her.

'She would be 83 now. Not many people born back then managed to make such an age.'

'I don't expect you to find her, but it would be nice to know her destiny. I hope she got to experience the richness of life as I have. There may have been more sadness than joy, but life isn't about keeping score. The brief moments when you experience the best of life vindicate the suffering at other times. Neither of us got that in our youth, but it would be good to know that she, like me, had that.'

It was several weeks before I saw Yuri again. He had left a message with one of the staff at the shop that he would be away for a while and would see me on his return to Saint Petersburg. He also told her to pass on that he would have some news for me when he returned.

When I did next see him, Dasha wasn't on my mind as much as the opportunity to chat with the one person who regularly talks to me. Before he said a word, he pulled a gift out of his bag and told me to unwrap it.

I could not believe it. Although I couldn't read any of what it said, it was a book, and on the cover was a photo of Dasha.

'It is called Hell and Heaven, From the Siege of Leningrad to the Land of the Free. It is her life story,' Yuri said. She migrated to America at the start of the 1950s. She got married to an American man named Simon and became Dasha Moore. That made her more unlikely ever to be tracked down, but I managed. She had three children and lived a relatively long, happy, healthy life. This book was written nearly twenty years ago.'

'And beyond this? What have you found out?'

'She died in 2008. I'm sorry.'

There was no great feeling of sadness with this news. It would have been a shock if she was still alive, and my great fears over what may have been had already been eased with Yuri's news and his gift for me.

'How can I get a version I can read?'

'It's not available in Russian, I'm afraid. I will have to come to your place and read it to you.'

He read the blurb and gave me a brief overview of the chapters, and it was clear that more than half of the book concentrated on our childhood traumas. From skimming through, Yuri could tell me that it included not just the time during the Siege but the period in the orphanage and under the care of the church. When she left the cathedral at age sixteen, she was living on the streets initially before she met a couple of people who were migrating to America. She applied and was granted the opportunity just after her eighteenth birthday. She settled in the Brighton Beach area of New York's Brooklyn borough, an area with a high concentration of Russian immigrants. She began working in a Russian restaurant. Simon worked in an adjacent building and was a regular customer, and in time, they built up a great rapport. He began providing her with the extra practice she needed to develop her English language skills, and she decided to use these to write her story.

Yuri told me he was free the following day if I wanted to hear the book. He was adamant that it was better to be done at home rather than in public, so I had him around to my apartment, a block away from Pyshechnaya.

It turned out that Yuri could read the entire book to me in a single day, long as it may have been. The first half centred on experiences I had shared with her, and while some of what she recounted didn't completely match my memories, most of it was a reasonable account of those traumatic years.

After detailing Babushka's death, she painted the picture of me being utterly dependent on her, which didn't connect with my recollection of us being a team. She was adamant that my inability to cope led to us being brought in by the authorities and ending up in the orphanage.

Her experiences at Nikolsky Cathedral vastly differed from what I endured. She was used, but not in the deviant nature that I endured. At the cathedral, the orphans were treated like slave labour, and while this was enough to make her desperately keen to leave when she turned sixteen, it hadn't been extreme enough to have her escape prematurely.

She wrote that her first aim when getting out was to find Anastasia and me, but she failed to do either. She recounted visiting the church I was at but was told that I had left. Given the timing, this wouldn't have been true, but knowing what else had been going on there, I have no reason to believe that Dasha was lying. She said that on a later trip to the church, she found it had been abandoned, and after investigating, she heard of some of the impropriety that had happened there. She feared that I may have been the one who paid the ultimate price. As the years passed, she had always just hoped it wasn't the case. Precisely as I had thought with her, we had lived in hope for each other.

Her life in America sounded idyllic. She found a welcoming community and, through their assistance, could find a job and housing quickly. She soon met the man with whom she would share her life, and it sounded like a perfect relationship. They were very much in love until she passed. Together, they had three children, all of whom had health and happiness, growing into successful adults with their own families. Her life was incredibly different to mine, and while envy was not a feeling I tended to allow myself, I was happy that she'd had that life rather than one like mine.

She wrestled with the idea of returning to the city of her birth so that she could give her children an appreciation of their heritage and good fortune for the time and place of their birth. Countering this desire was a level of fear at the memories she would be bringing up. Once she started writing the book, she felt she had to see the city again, albeit a very different city with a different name. Her husband, her adult children, their spouses, and their two grandchildren all made the journey.

The greatest highlight of her trip, the book says, was after more than half a century, she got to meet her sister, Anastasia. The great lowlight of the book followed shortly after, as Anastasia then told her that she had never found me and believed I had been killed as part of a sequence of killings associated with orphans at the Church of the Resurrection. Anastasia knew that was a lie after meeting me in the mid-1970s. It made no sense that she would say this, stopping Dasha from looking for me. In all likelihood, we were unlikely ever to find each other, but that wasn't relevant. Hope carries a value of its own. What possible reason could she have had for taking hope away from her sister? I had not understood Anastasia's attitude then, but this was far more hurtful and impossible to understand.

The book finished with an overview of the fine lines that constitute life. She focussed on the miracle that the three of us somehow survived when most of our family died in the Siege. On how two of us were sent to different church-run homes, one of which was almost a death camp, while the other was set on a path that led her to a new life. Throughout her time in America, she continued to have luck go her way when so many people around her faced various devastation.

After completing the book, Yuri showed me some printouts he had done online that were printed after she died. One included an interview in a local American paper, where she had said that her greatest sadness in life was not being able to save her cousin Ekaterina, who had depended on her.

'She carried you with her forever. It would be best to take that from the story, not anything about Anastasia,' Yuri said.

I had shed tears in a few places throughout the book. It wasn't a regular thing for me, immune as I essentially was to be grieving after all that I'd experienced early in life. I guess the book had returned me to that point, exposing me again to the little girl who had hoped for so much 80 years ago.

'Come with me, Yuri. If I'm going to feel better now, I need pyshki.'

CHAPTER 39

January 6, 2022

ADAM

Today, we would say goodbye to Russia, flying out this evening from Pulkovo Airport to our next destination, the Finnish capital of Helsinki. The tour is officially over, with everyone leaving at different times today. We have two other people travelling with us to the airport tonight. Cherie is also on the flight to Helsinki, transferring there to a flight to Berlin, while Jeremy is flying to Amsterdam.

We saw Carol and Jeff when we went down to breakfast. They were just about to leave for their midday flight back to the United States, and it was good to have the opportunity to say goodbye. Before returning to our room to begin the now-familiar task of packing up and preparing for checkout, we were stopped at the reception desk. A parcel had been delivered for us. We hadn't been expecting anything, so it was with great surprise that we looked at each other, and Louise motioned for me to open it.

Inside was a coffee-table style book that appeared to be a tribute to Saint Petersburg. The cover was written in Cyrillic, so I asked the clerk at the reception if she could read it for me.

'A Home By Any Name, Ekaterina Komarova.'

On the back was a photo of a younger Ekaterina, from what I estimated would have been twenty years earlier. With the book was a letter for us.

Adam and Louise,

Ekaterina had wanted to put together her favourite works in a collection many years ago, and with a bit of assistance, I was able to get this book published. Only a small run was printed, so you're never likely to find a copy in your part of the world. You have a truly unique souvenir of this city to take home. She is an amazing woman. I am glad you got to see that, and I am so happy that she got the joy of sharing that.

People tend to make assumptions at first sight, and while that sometimes may spare them an inconvenient encounter, it more frequently costs them a rare opportunity. Many of the most amazing stories stem from what may appear to be the most uninteresting-looking people.

I never knew my parents. I was left at a Leningrad orphanage around the same time Ekaterina had her son. As I have lived a similarly lonely life, she has filled that void for me while I have done the same for her. We are both private enough people that our interactions in Pyshechnaya define much of our relationship, and it always has. We met there by chance, and familiarity by sight led to conversation. Only after an extended time were the level of connections understood. You were able to establish her life story straight away. Nobody else has done that, and now you're among the few to know how incredible that life story has been.

On her birthday next week, she will go to Pyshechnaya like every other day. She will clear trays and rubbish because it is what she does. She will get stared at by some, ignored by most and most likely acknowledged by nobody but me. In amongst all of that, she will carry the memory of your visit and will be overjoyed for that.

Thank you, and safe travels.

Yuri and Ekaterina.

Once again, we were both in tears.

'What time are we going there today?' Louise asked.

'I was hoping you'd say that.' We hadn't planned too much for the day, so with spare time, we could drop in and hopefully see her again.

We couldn't communicate without Yuri, but all that was left to say to her didn't need words.

We wanted to return to the hotel by 4, giving ourselves time for a drink in the bar and an extra buffer before our car was scheduled to take us to the airport. Anything else high on our wish list for our time in the city had already been done, but I had an idea.

'I think we should recreate some of the photos from her book. They're not going to look so professional, but how cool would it be to flick through her book and have a collection of our photos that match it? We can then tell her story and connect with our pictures showing how we traced her steps.'

'They're from right across the city. We don't have time for that,' Louise said.

'I'm not talking the whole book, just a couple of shots, anywhere we happen to be nearby.'

We sat in the lobby and briefly flicked through the book. Louise did a quick Google search of the book title and Ekaterina's name, but nothing came up. This had been a very limited-release book. We couldn't identify the publisher with all the wording in Cyrillic script, but Lila was in the hotel assisting everyone as they were checking out, so we went over and gained her insight.

'This is cool,' she said, looking at the book. 'I would say this is the late 1990s, looking at the skyline.'

I went back to the start, showing that it was published in 1998 and asked if she could tell us who the publisher was.

'Fiorevsky. But that mightn't help you much. Nearly 25 years later, the chances of a small publisher still being around is minimal.'

'The photographer is the woman we met downtown that I told you about the other day,' I explained. 'We got sent this without any idea such a book existed. We don't have a way of tracking her down to say thank you. We wanted to recreate one of the photos and send it to her and thought the publisher might be the best way.'

'When someone shows generosity, they rarely do it to get something in return. I'm sure her wish would be for you to appreciate the book, nothing more,' Lila said.

'True, but how does she know that her wish for us to appreciate it has come true?'

'Faith doesn't need to be about religion. If she has survived the type of life you mentioned, she doesn't need to see something to believe it.'

I understood what she meant. I still would always prefer to see appreciation for a gift I had given rather than blindly believing it. Perhaps that meant that nothing I ever gave was unconditional, for I always wanted something in return. It might not be material, but it was still a desire.

We returned to our rooms, finished packing, and then returned downstairs to check out. Lila was there, still finishing with Cherie, who had beaten us to reception. Once they finished, we asked Cherie about her plans for the day. Like us, she had been uncertain but decided to go to New Holland Island for outdoor ice skating with Jeremy.

'Jeremy again,' Louise said with a smirk. 'What happened last night?'

Cherie smiled, then looked away, before changing topics. She swapped numbers with Louise so they could contact each other if they ran out of options throughout the day. If we hadn't seen each other before, we agreed to meet at the hotel for a drink at 4 pm.

Once Lila was free, we collected our passports from her, which had to be maintained in the hotel safe from check-in until check-out under Russian regulations. She had been a great tour guide, and we thanked her for her organisation, patience, and professionalism, as well as giving her a generous gratuity.

'And thank you for being such enthusiastic tourists. I am glad you have enjoyed our beautiful country so much,' she said.

It's true. It was a beautiful country, and we enjoyed every moment here. For all of its attractions and the unique experiences it offered, I was sure that my strongest memories of Russia would always relate to an old-style doughnut shop and what our times there connected to.

CHAPTER 40

January 2, 2022

EKATERINA

So next week I turn eighty-eight. What is left for me?

I looked at Yuri, content that I had finished my story, and he told the Australians accordingly.

'Your story so far,' Adam said.

I laughed when Yuri translated his words.

'Who knows how long is left, but at this age, there isn't the volume of experiences that each day brings a younger person.'

They believed my story to be tragic, the tears having welled in their eyes on multiple occasions and still evident in the woman's eyes.

'What is wrong?' I got Yuri to ask her.

'It's just such a rich yet sad story,' she said.

'It's a rich story, but not all sad,' Yuri replied. 'Ekaterina views her life as a triumph. She wakes up grateful every day.'

'Yes, but enjoying a doughnut, or should I say pyshki, is not compensation for rape, losing a child, having her family killed around her,' Adam said.

Yuri translated this back to me, and I explained as best I could.

'There is no scoreboard in life. How many positives, how many negatives, how much is each of these worth? None of us did anything to earn our place on this earth. We were all the result of a miracle. From that moment, everything that happens combines various factors, few of which remain within our control. We do our best with these but understand that everything else will shape our lives more. Look at every other species we share this planet with. The mayfly lives for just one day before dying. Millions of different creatures are food for other animals and learn from day one that they are in a battle for survival, lest they be gone soon after.

'Maybe most humans have not experienced my losses, but they then haven't learnt the ability to appreciate the little things as I have. You have had to fly halfway around the world to come here and experience something so new and different. I get every bit as much joy and thrill from waking up under a roof, looking outside at the sunrise, the clouds, the snow, the canals, the flowers and the manufactured miracles that line the streets of this city.

'I have two arms and legs that have functioned my whole life. I have heart complications, but despite the threat that it would kill me, I'm still here, and it has never really impacted me. I can see, I can hear, I can smell, I can taste. For the past 75 years, at least, I have never gone hungry.

'I may be 88 next week, but I still say that life is short. I don't have time to waste. Bemoaning what you don't have is a waste of time when you could use that time to find the best way to use what you do have. Part of what makes any moment the best is appreciating the best parts of it.'

The woman was crying even more now.

'I feel so....... I don't know what words to use,' she said.

'Ungrateful?' her husband added.

'Yes.'

'Spasiba,' the man said to me before returning to Yuri, needing his more detailed thanks to be translated from his native tongue.

'She is inspiring. I think it's a lesson for people like us to learn to appreciate the little moments more. Being here, we appreciate every moment, but when you're not exposed to new and exciting experiences daily, there is still so much to appreciate.'

I nodded my head as Yuri repeated his words in Russian. 'Everyone has a story,' I said. 'You don't need inspiration from an old woman in Russia. It exists within yourselves, your families and friends.'

'None of them have had experiences like you, Ekaterina,' he said.

'Then you have missed one of the main points. Life isn't about your experiences as much as it is about what you make from those experiences. That is your story. That is your legacy.'

I'm not used to these conversations. Besides Yuri, nobody has listened to me for so long that I haven't been used to telling anyone what I think. These people have hung on my every word. Maybe they'll forget it all tomorrow, but at least I feel like it is an opportunity to pass on what I know of life.

While living in the basement through the Siege, I asked my mama what the meaning of life was, feeling so torn by how the world was crumbling around us.

'To do whatever we can to make the world a better place,' she said.

When she'd left us, and I told this story to Babushka, explaining how her death had proven that she didn't make the world a better place, she helped me interpret the concept differently.

'How we make the world a better place varies for us all,' she said. 'For Mr Stalin, it may have been defeating the Nazis. For your mama, it was by teaching you the lessons that can help you grow into a woman who understands the world's needs better than people like Stalin ever could.

'Our actions can improve the world, but so can the words we write, the pictures we paint, the lessons we teach, the people we help. Maybe you will one day meet someone and share with them something that only you can. Maybe that person then changes the world or inspires the next person to do the same.'

Eighty years on, I wondered if this was true. These tourists do not seem like the future leaders who will shape the world, but therein lies the mystery. Maybe someone hears their story, and if they've included part of mine, the story goes on. As long as it gets heard, somewhere, someday, it may help make the world a better place.

They offered to buy me more pyshki, but I wanted nothing more. They asked if there was anything they could do for me or Yuri, so grateful they were for the couple of hours we had spent with them, but neither of us wanted anything. The satisfaction of having someone listen to me rather than stare at me was enough. Yuri was similarly happy to see me like this.

They said their goodbyes after briefly interacting about the city's highlights. The main attractions were on their agenda, so I had little to add. I said I hoped they experienced the whole magic of this city and could return one day and see the other Saint Petersburg, the city as it is during the White Nights.

I turned to Yuri and thanked him for playing the role of translator.

'You're welcome, of course. I was slightly surprised you didn't tell them about me,' he said.

'In such a complicated story, I felt it better not to add that extra level.'

Yuri was born in Saint Petersburg in 1947. He was one of thousands of babies abandoned at an orphanage in the city in that era. Through a casual conversation in Pyshechnaya forty years later, he discovered that I had given birth as an orphan and had left the baby where he grew up. Soon after I escaped the church in 1949, I discovered I was pregnant. With Irena's support, I had the child, but there was never any question about me keeping him. I left him at the orphanage, accepting there was no way I could raise him. I never told Borislav about him. Even after losing both Yegveny and Borsilav, I never sought to find him, though there was a part of me that always hoped that he may choose to find me. It never happened, but I don't think it could have ever led to a better relationship than what I have had with Yuri.

'You know it is not possible Yuri. Aside from anything else, you are two years too old.'

'Maybe my birth certificate was wrong. Or your memory?'
'Never.'

I had told him this thirty years ago, but as time passed, we built a relationship that was of value, nonetheless. We may not be mother and son, but my relationship with him was better than most women my age would have with their sons.

What Yuri gained in return was a little harder to know. Beyond anything else, I think he wanted the belief that someone would be there for him through thick and thin, and he believed I was that person. I certainly wasn't going anywhere. Perhaps he genuinely believed I was his mother, though I think it is far more likely he accepted the truth but used me as a symbol of his mother. He always called me Ekaterina. I wouldn't have been comfortable with anything else. To anyone who sees us here, it is a strange friendship and nothing else. He is always spoken of as a friend when he has accompanied me to appointments. When my will was done, he was explained similarly. This was the best anyone could do when you have no next of kin. He would not have worried when we found out about Dasha and her children, for there was little I had to pass on. Yuri was in a strong enough financial position that it wouldn't matter to him anyway. It was predominantly symbolic, but after all these years, my link with Yuri was my truest.

We didn't see too much of each other outside of Pyshechnaya. Occasionally, one of us would visit the other's home, but our twice-weekly catchups over pyshki were usually sufficient. Since he retired, I have felt more comfortable asking for his time when necessary, but such independence formed through the nature of my life tends to dominate the way I operate, so this hasn't become common.

'I should go home and have a lie-down, Yuri.'

'Are you alright?' he asked.

'Yes. I'm just not used to going through so much all in one sitting. As stoic as I am, I feel slightly drained.'

Yuri walked me back to my apartment building before heading back in the opposite direction to his home. He had been the person closest to me for over half of my life. I'd tried to push him away with the certainty that he couldn't be my son, yet his persistence had led to building the relationship. As insignificant as it may seem to people with family and friends, it has proven invaluable. Yuri is the only person I have on an ongoing basis, though it doesn't mean that it is the only way people play a role in my life.

People need people. We don't necessarily all need them in the same ways, but very few people ever shake this natural need completely. Throughout life, I have continued to lose people I wanted to keep and to run away and hide from the rest. It never meant I didn't need people. I just needed them in different ways. As technology has allowed it, people communicate with each other more than ever before, yet they do so more frequently from a distance. I have worked in the opposite way, rarely communicating but feeling the need to have people around me. My tastebuds and the symbolism first took me to Pyshechnaya, but the people kept me returning. I needed a place where I would be surrounded by strangers. There is no commitment on my part, but there is the opportunity to see people, observe them and gain an understanding of them. In the shop, we see all types, young and old, locals and tourists, and it becomes a busy cross-section of the modern world. When I am there, it is the one time that I feel like I am part of a community, a feeling I value highly.

CHAPTER 41

January 6, 2022

ADAM

'Well, of course, pyshki is part of the deal,' I said as we walked down Nevsky Prospect on our way to Pyshechnaya. We hoped to see Ekaterina but knew she wasn't there constantly. I maintained that some pyshki for lunch would be satisfactory if we got nothing else.

Souvenir stalls were set up alongside the canal, just down from the Church on Spilled Blood. As tempted as I was to rummage through looking for mementos of our time here, I knew that Ekaterina's book was an infinitely superior option to anything I would find. Louise had already bought some Matryoshka dolls to take home as presents for people when we were in Moscow, so there wasn't a need.

'The photography came up several times, but she never really said what she did with it. I can't believe there was such an amazing book out there. I also can't believe that her cousin could have also had a book out, and with two published authors, they never found each other,' Louise said.

'Whatever you are looking for is much harder to find once you stop looking. Well, certainly once you close your eyes, and I think Dasha's eyes would not have been open to Ekaterina.'

'What would the difference have been? As she said, circumstance creates a situation for you, and the quality of life comes from what you do with the situation. She didn't need anyone more at that point in life.'

I nodded but continued to compare Ekaterina's thought processes to mine. I understood her philosophy, but surely it was reasonable to wish for better circumstances. The lesson was not to dwell on lesser circumstances once they'd passed.

We came to Bolshaya Konyushennaya and walked down towards what had become the most familiar building in the city to us. Perhaps this old shop didn't have the fame of the Hermitage or Saint Isaacs, but to us, it symbolised something equally memorable.

'There weren't any photos of Pyshechnaya or its products in the book, was there?' I said, sure that it would have stood out enough for me not to miss.

'No, but considering the beauty around this city, do you think it should be?'

'Depends on how you define beauty. Love is beautiful, and this place has been the love of her life or at least a large section of it.'

'I think she wanted to pay tribute to her city as a photographer, not produce a memoir. If it was her story, I'm sure you would have seen a little more pyshki.'

'But Ekaterina's story is the story of Saint Petersburg,' I said.

'There may not be anyone who personifies everything about this city the way she does, but it still doesn't make their stories the same.'

True as her words were, the parallels seemed inescapable to me. The more we get to know a person, the more we understand the complete picture of who they are. In all the years that Louise and I have been together, there are still things we learn. Expecting to fully understand Ekaterina's story from an hour-long explanation is ludicrous. The same applies to places, and a few days in this city gives us a snapshot. The snapshot of the person and place makes it look like they tell the same story, though it is probably more accurate to suggest that they fit within the same genre.

Walking in the door of Pyshechnaya for the last time, we immediately scoured the room but couldn't see Ekaterina.

'C'mon, I will grab some pyshki. Who knows, she may turn up while we eat them.'

I now felt comfortable with the ordering process despite my Russian not having developed in the previous few days. We decided to forgo the coffee this time, having decided that two previous times of not liking something was enough of an indication that some things weren't meant to be.

It was comparatively quiet in the café, so we could get a table with chairs close by the door so we would not miss her if she walked in. It was almost driven by a desire to stay as long as possible, but I ate my pyshki incredibly slowly.

'What more could you have done if you saw her again?'

'Nothing,' I said. 'I guess to thank her for the book, but it is just that bit of human nature that always wants to recapture the best moments one more time.' I shrugged my shoulders and admitted it didn't matter.

'Sometimes your words and expressions are a long way apart,' Louise said. Naturally, she knew me well enough to know what I thought without the need for me to say it. Sometimes, I felt compelled to verbalise agreement, even if she wouldn't believe it.

'So where to?' I asked, eyeing the last pyshki on the plate.

'We still have money on our Podorozhnik cards, so there's no issue going out anywhere on the subway.'

Subways here could be travelled all day for the cost of one fare. You only paid on entering the station at the start of your journey. You could do a tour of every one of the city's seventy-two stations for about forty rubles. Still, if you got out and walked around the block before coming back underground, you'd continue paying forty rubles each time you entered a station.

'I reckon we go and look at New Holland Island a bit later,' Louise said. 'We can walk back to the hotel from there, so it's just a case of whether we do anything else before that.'

'Maybe we just wander down Nevsky again. Wouldn't mind walking through Palace Square again, get one more look at some of the city's highlights, then we can go to New Holland Park, I guess.'

I wouldn't say I liked schedules like the one we had today. When we planned the trip, I hated flying out of places early in the morning because it impacted the night before as much as anything else. I reasoned that an evening departure meant we effectively had a full day in Saint Petersburg to do as we pleased. Still, the whole day inevitably felt like we were watching the clock, conscious that time dictated anything we wanted to do. We could find things to do here for months, but everything we felt we needed to do had been done before today. In hindsight, I would have preferred to have left mid to late morning and had the afternoon and evening to explore the Finnish capital on arrival.

You learn from every experience when you travel. There isn't a golden rule about the best options as it differs for each person, and in many cases, it can vary for the same people in different circumstances. In the middle of our German stay, we went through five cities in six days. The theory was that we travelled just after hotel check-out time, arriving in the next town at hotel check-in time, and ended up seeing cities we otherwise would have bypassed. It seemed like the perfect plan, but the reality wasn't so golden. While there was an advantage to seeing more, we appreciated less. You arrived in a city knowing you had only minimal time there, so you were out exploring as much as you could as quickly as you could. Before too long, we were drained, and we realised we did not need to see as much but needed to appreciate more.

I was just about to pick up my backpack and get up when the door opened.

'Ekaterina,' I called out.

CHAPTER 42

January 6, 2022

EKATERINA

Just like every day, as I approached the door, I could hear Babushka's voice in my head as clearly as it had been eighty years earlier. She was again talking about the girl with the magical plate who closed her eyes and wished for it to be filled by pyshki, then opened them to see her wish had come true. It was an automatic thought for me to close my eyes as I opened the door, so the moment I set foot inside, the sense of smell took over, and I could breathe in that intoxicating aroma. That always brings me greater peace than the ensuing taste ever achieves when I get to eat one. I enjoy the taste, but the memories of innocence, the basement and Babushka are captured and squeezed close to my heart before I reach that point.

It is often noisy when I walk in, but the particular noise I hear first takes me by surprise.

'Ekaterina,' I hear, called out in a heavy accent that I would have thought was English a few days ago but now knew as Australian. The couple from the other day were back again. I hope they knew Yuri was never here on a Thursday, so they had little chance of asking questions.

I went over to the table in the corner where they were standing. As I approached, the man took a book out of his backpack—my book. Yuri had managed to do as I requested.

'*Bolshoye spasiba*,' he said, sounding more Russian to his ears than mine. I knew it was an attempt to show me he appreciated the gift. He placed the book on the table, put his hands on his heart, lowered his head in a nodding motion, and then pointed back to the book. He demonstrated something I have long known: you do not always need words to communicate.

They both loved the book. The woman flicked through and pointed to a photo of the Alexander Garden under a heavy blanket of snow, with the golden dome of Saint Isaacs peeking through a gap between the trees. Like her husband, she placed her hand on her heart to indicate her love of that photo. She flicked further into the book and repeated the same gesture after finding a shot from Avtovo Station. She then moved on to the back of the book, pointing to a photo looking west along Nevsky Prospect.

The man held out his hand to say stop or wait before using some awkward hand signals to indicate that he would go out the back and order some pyshki and drinks. Now, it was my turn to nod and put my hand on my heart as an expression of thanks.

While we waited for him, I pointed out my three favourite photos from the book. None were such prominent places, but I was proud of the composition. The first was a canal at night, just a couple of blocks away from Palace Square, with the lights from the adjacent apartment buildings shimmering on the water. The next was a shot of an old man and a young woman arguing their respective sides of the debate at the 1991 protests in Saint Isaacs Square.

Unsurprisingly, the third of my favourite photos was taken outside the door here. People staring in the window to see what the fuss was about, and the resident cat of the day, Misha, staring back at them.

The woman took out her camera and showed it to me. I couldn't imagine such an advanced piece of equipment. I wondered how much more I could have done as a photographer half a century later. She took a photo of the main part of the shop and then tried to show me what she'd taken. My eyesight was not good enough to look through her viewer. As her husband returned with coffee and pyshki, it seemed she wanted to take a photo of him and me together, but I shook my head. I have only ever wanted to be on the other side of the camera.

'*Tebe ne nuzhna moya fotografiya, chtoby pomnit menya.*' I told her she didn't need a photo to remember me. She did not understand, but her husband seemed to. It wasn't the words but the perception. After he said something to her, she smiled and held her heart again.

He pointed to his watch, and I knew it was time to say goodbye. I nodded and moved, picking up the tray to dispose of the waste and clear the table for others. I don't know if they wanted an emotional farewell, but I don't do such things. I waved my hand and walked towards the back section, sending the cat scurrying to avoid me. I turned around, and the man was still looking at me, a tear formed in his eye. He is a strange man, but a good one, I believe. I smile again and raise my hand. He nods and, with his wife, turns and walks to the door.

Perhaps our communication had been limited without the ability to talk, but how important is most of what people say? Most of what we need to communicate is how we feel. Words can assist in doing this, but they are not essential. Being human, we learn how to show these feelings and how to see them. Sometimes, we don't even realise we have these skills, but when we need them, they are there.

This city is unique. I guess every city is, but the uniqueness is far more evident here than in most places. From Saint Petersburg to Petrograd, then Leningrad before returning to the original name. A rose by any other name is meant to smell as sweet, but our name changes have matched significant changes. We went from one of the most dynamic cities in the world in earlier centuries to becoming the bastion of tragedy and gloom with the change to Leningrad. When we returned to the original name, we again changed back towards being an envied city. The name changes haven't been the cause, but there is more than coincidence involved. Carrying the name of Peter, it has been progressive, creative and inspiring like the man it is named for.

In this city, people's understanding of limits is very different. Here, we spend months of the year looking at sunlight at midnight. Later, we experience darkness through most of the day. Beyond anything else, that already sets the scene for a range of mindsets different to what is experienced in most places.

Analysing people always leaves questions about the relative significance of nature and nurture. The same approach can be taken when looking at cities. How much of what defines Saint Petersburg stems from our geography, and how much of it is based on our history? No doubt, both have played a role to some degree. Both of these are so completely unique that it is inevitable that this city is one of a kind.

For all the change the city has seen, a spirit underpins all the extremes. In the ultimate battle that defined World War II, Hitler aimed not just to destroy our city but to obliterate the innocent citizens and give them no way out. Stalin, his ultimate rival, was largely disinterested in saving us. He was more than willing to sacrifice the city and its people for his idea of the greater good. It was circumstance rather than the Soviet regime that led to the heroism that played such a role in changing history.

In amongst the tragedy, it may seem hard to believe that a ring-shaped piece of fried dough could have such an impact on a life. For years, pyshki meant innocence. It meant happiness. It meant sharing with loved ones. It meant hope.

Everything I lost and yearned to experience seemed to connect to the pyshki. Even after all these years, the pyshki had led to my story getting told to people from the other side of the world. For a moment, I meant something to someone else, another of those ongoing yearnings.

I wouldn't wish the circumstances I've lived through on anyone, yet those circumstances define my life. I can't change them. There is no me without them, so while I reflect on each tragedy with sadness and bitterness, these emotions relate purely to the events themselves. They do not overwhelm me and remove me from the positivity I feel about life. If anything, enduring so much pain has meant I see the beauty in the world far more clearly than most people. That is why I am so good at photography. Without the tragedies, would I have had that same appreciation of the beauty in life?

I want to think that our species learns from its mistakes, and we shall never see such a horror as World War II again. I am far from optimistic that this is true. In every conflict, there is net suffering, but there is also a minority who gain from it. At some point, someone with enough power will consider their potential gains to justify suffering in others. Our President was born and raised in this city, but I do not doubt he'd inflict the same suffering on any group if he thought it was in his best interests.

We understand the impact of rape, but it still happens. We know the effects of persecution, but it still happens. People continue to put themselves, their fraternity and their causes above the common good. Sometimes, they believe it is the common good they are acting for. In doing so, they often commit evil without even knowing it is what they are doing. The person at the bottom suffers, just as my family and I did. Fortunately, I found my way out of a situation few people would.

You must struggle at the lowest depths to appreciate the view at the top of the highest peaks. As a city, we had done this well; nobody typified this more than me.

There is so much beauty in life when you are looking for it correctly. Where each person finds it will differ, even in a golden circle of fried dough.

Also by C.R.Page

Bedside in Berlin
Paradox in Paris
Hurdles in Hobart
Torches in Tokyo
The Ride to Work

www.ingramcontent.com/pod-product-compliance
Lightning Source LLC
Chambersburg PA
CBHW020511120726
47904CB00003B/789